Readers love
L.A. WITT

Wrenches, Regrets, & Reality Checks

"L.A. Witt did a wonderful job on this short story and I look forward to more books in the Wrench Wars series."

—Gay Book Reviews

"I absolutely adored this book. Wes is so cute and Reggie is just plain hot. They might've looked like opposites from the outside but they were perfect together."
—Rainbow Book Reviews

Last Mechanic Standing

"L.A. Witt never disappoints with her books and this one doesn't either!"

—Diverse Reader

"…this was an extremely enjoyable read, packed with angst, romance, sweetness, chemistry, hot sex, but mostly love."

—Bayou Book Junkie

By L.A. WITT

Rules of Engagement • Rain

TUCKER SPRINGS
Where Nerves End

WRENCH WARS
Last Mechanic Standing
By Marie Sexton: Normal Enough
Wrenches, Regrets, & Reality Checks
By Marie Sexton: Making Waves
With Marie Sexton: Wrench Wars Anthology

Published by DREAMSPINNER PRESS
www.dreamspinnerpress.com

WHERE NERVES END

L.A. WITT

Published by
DREAMSPINNER PRESS

5032 Capital Circle SW, Suite 2, PMB# 279,
Tallahassee, FL 32305-7886 USA
www.dreamspinnerpress.com

Where Nerves End
© 2018 L.A. Witt.

Cover Art
© 2018 Reese Dante.
http://www.reesedante.com
Cover content is for illustrative purposes only and any person depicted
on the cover is a model.

Mass Market ISBN: 978-1-64108-125-2
Trade Paperback ISBN: 978-1-64080-900-0
Digital ISBN: 978-1-64080-899-7
Library of Congress Control Number: 2018906777
Mass Market Paperback published November 2018
v. 1.0
First Edition published by Amber Quill Press, LLC, June 2012.
Second Edition published by Riptide Publishing, June 2014.

Printed in the United States of America
∞
This paper meets the requirements of
ANSI/NISO Z39.48-1992 (Permanence of Paper).

Acknowledgments

THANK YOU to Marie Sexton, for putting up with me for that weekend when I'd sprained my wrist and decided to flee Nebraska for a few days, which gave us the opportunity to dream up what would eventually become Tucker Springs.

Also to Dr. B. and Dr. J. for everything they taught me about acupuncture, both from letting me pick their brains and from my own treatments. This book wouldn't exist without everything I learned from both of you.

Chapter 1

ONE NIGHT without pain didn't seem like too much to ask. Just eight goddamned hours of uninterrupted unconsciousness. No scalding-hot showers at three fifteen. No forcing back nausea long enough to throw down a few pills. No waking up convinced I'd been run over by a truck.

One. Night.

Either it really was too much to ask or I was asking the wrong deity, because I was awake again. And tonight, the pain was *excruciating*.

A white-hot blade extending from my left collarbone to the back of my shoulder had jarred me out of a semisound sleep. It didn't matter how many times this happened, it always startled me, and it always made my eyes water.

Biting back curses, I carefully freed myself from Kyle's—Kevin's?—arms and gingerly sat up. Once I was upright, I took a few slow, deep breaths until the pain subsided enough for me to focus my eyes.

The alarm clock said a little past five, which meant I'd been asleep for less than an hour. Now that was just cruel, damn it.

I needed a hot shower. I got up, moving carefully and quietly so I wouldn't wake up… whatever his name was.

In the shower, I closed my eyes and breathed while the water—turned as hot as I could stand—beat on my shoulder. My doctor insisted on ice instead of heat, but fuck that. Ice made the spasms worse.

After ten solid minutes under the hot water, the pain receded a little. I tried to find comfort in that minor relief, but I knew better. As soon as I was out of the shower, the pain would come right back, sinking unseen teeth into my left shoulder.

Slowly releasing my breath, I focused on my game plan. Once the water stopped, I'd have less than five minutes to get downstairs, eat something, and take a painkiller. Any longer than that and the spasms would have a chance to move back in before I could head them off at the pass. As long as I could do it in that time, I stood a small chance of getting some sleep.

In theory, anyway.

Toweling off was never a pleasant procedure with a fucked-up shoulder. I dried myself enough to keep from dripping all over the hardwood floors—slipping and busting my ass wouldn't help matters.

I just hoped to God I could get to the painkillers before the spasms came back, especially since it sometimes hurt bad enough to nauseate me. That complicated the whole "eat a few bites and take a pill" part of the equation.

I wrapped the towel around my waist and headed downstairs. In the kitchen, I flicked on the light above the stove. I wasn't big on convenience food, but I kept things like bagels around specifically for when I needed to take a pain pill. Something quick that wouldn't aggravate the nausea that showed up on the worst nights. Nights like this.

I'd have kept it all upstairs, along with the painkillers, but I'd convinced myself that if I had to wake up completely and come all the way down to the kitchen instead of popping a pill while I was half asleep, then I'd only take them when I absolutely needed to.

In theory.

I settled on half a bagel, and while I slowly, carefully ate that, I stared down the bottle of pills the same way I did every time this happened.

Is it really bad enough tonight, Jason?

Can you suck it up and sleep on it?

Do you really *need this?*

I rolled my shoulder, and the motion carved bright red lines along my collarbone and through the muscles. My eyes stung, and for a couple of seconds I couldn't even draw a breath. Yeah, I needed the pill.

I swallowed it. In a few minutes I'd go back to bed, and with any luck the drug would kick in before sunrise. Hopefully it would at least take the edge off; I'd been using this shit so long, I was building up a tolerance, and it helped less and less every time. My doctor had suggested a higher dose or a stronger narcotic, but I'd balked. I was dependent enough already.

Sighing, I rested my hands on the counter and slowly tilted my head, trying to stretch the muscles across my shoulder blade. Not that it ever helped, but that didn't stop me from trying.

Something had to change besides my painkiller dosage. I had a business to run, a life to live. Lack of sleep and an abundance of pain interfered with every goddamned thing from driving my car to enjoying my sad excuse for a sex life.

Pursing my lips, I glanced at the stairs leading up to my bedroom where Kevin—no, I was pretty sure his name was Kyle—was still asleep. Just once, it would be nice to have sex with someone without having to modify everything we did to keep from aggravating my shoulder. Nothing killed the mood or took the luster off an orgasm quite like fierce, unrelenting pain. I couldn't even enjoy rough sex anymore because I spent the whole time worrying that our pursuit of good pain would trigger the not-so-good pain. Sex wasn't very appealing when this was the end result.

But Kyle had given me that look while I was getting ready to close the club last night, and it hadn't taken me long to decide, *Oh, what the hell?* He was cute, he was aggressive, and he was a damned good kisser. When I could hear him over the music, he'd whispered the *filthiest* things in my ear. One flirty hand over the front of my pants and I'd stopped trying to talk myself out of it.

I rubbed my shoulder, silently begging the spasms not to spread up my neck or down my back before the drugs kicked in.

This had to stop. I couldn't live like this.

"You know," my friend Seth's voice echoed in my head, "I keep telling you—"

"I'll pass on the acupuncture. If I'm going to spend money, I'd rather spend it on something that actually helps, you know?"

"Suit yourself," he'd said with a shrug and gone back to working on my tattoo. "But if you change your mind, give me a buzz and I'll hook you up with a guy who can help."

In the silence of my kitchen, I closed my eyes and kneaded the back of my neck as the stiffness crept upward. For the first time, I was truly tempted to get that number from Seth.

But then there was money. All the worsening financial problems that kept me awake when my shoulder didn't. Things had been spiraling out of control since I'd lost my business partner last year, and it hadn't gotten any better when Wes moved out, taking his half of the mortgage payment with him. Ironically, my relentless pain had been one of the catalysts for our breakup, and the breakup had created more problems, which had stressed me out enough to make my shoulder worse. If irony were a painkiller, I wouldn't have this damned ongoing Percocet prescription.

The muscles knotted tighter. The tension climbed higher, inching toward my hairline and clawing its way around to the other side of my neck. Stiffness coiled around my spine, descending toward the middle of my back. The more I worried, the more it hurt. The more it hurt, the more I worried.

To hell with it. Tomorrow I'd get that number from Seth. I really couldn't afford it, but oh fucking well. Maybe the acupuncture would help.

I prayed to anyone who'd listen that it would.

BY THE grace of God and coffee, I was able to drive safely the next morning. Cameron, as his name turned out to be, lived on the other side of town, and since I was headed that way anyway, I took him home.

As my car idled in front of his apartment building, he grinned and said, "Give me a call if you ever want a rematch."

I returned the grin. "Bet on it."

He made no move to kiss me, just winked and got out of the car. I hadn't decided yet if I'd call him. Probably not. He certainly wasn't lacking in bed, but I wasn't interested in much beyond a one-night stand right now. Maintaining a relationship was a bitch when someone started equating "my shoulder hurts too much" with "I have a headache." Casual sex with men whose names I barely knew was less stressful.

After I'd left Cameron's apartment, I pulled into another parking lot and dialed Seth's cell phone. Surprise, surprise, it went straight to voicemail. That meant he was either working on someone or fucking someone. Probably the former, since Saturdays were the shop's busiest days.

I set my phone on the passenger seat, turned onto the main road, and headed over to the Light District. This was the town's unofficial gay neighborhood. Seattle had Capitol Hill. San Francisco had the Castro District. Tucker Springs had the Light District.

At ten o'clock on a Saturday morning, the streets weren't that busy. Once more shops and the breweries opened around the cobblestone town square and along the narrow side streets, the place would be crawling with locals and tourists alike. For now, it was mostly deserted.

It was here, half a block from the tourist magnet town square and not far from my nightclub, that Seth had set up his tattoo shop. Sitting under a couple of loft apartments, Ink Springs fit in surprisingly well with the old-style brick storefronts of the New Age shop and the used bookstore on either side. It was a far cry from one of those shady, grungy shops in the more questionable parts of town, and Seth had gone for a tasteful sign that didn't stick out like a rock-band T-shirt at a black-tie gathering.

The Open sign in the window was dim, but the shop lights were on. I parked between Seth's beat-up red Chevy S10 and a gray sedan, then went to the door.

It was locked, but Seth looked up from working on the back of a guy lying facedown on one of the black leather tables. Seth gave a sharp nod and set his tattoo gun aside. He said something to his client, then came across the shop, peeling off his rubber gloves as he walked.

He turned the dead bolt and let me in. "Hey, Jason. I wasn't expecting you."

"Yeah, sorry to bug you at work," I said as he locked the door behind me. "I, um, I wanted to ask you about that acupuncturist friend of yours."

Seth's eyes widened. "You're actually going to call him?"

"I... maybe."

He grimaced. "Bad night?"

"Real bad." I chewed my lip. "You really believe in the stuff he does?"

"Absolutely," he said without hesitation. "Hand to God, it's—"

"Oh, *that's* meaningful coming from an atheist heathen."

He laughed. "What can I say? But I swear, the shit works like a damned charm. It drives me fucking crazy too. It shouldn't work. It doesn't make a bit of sense, but"—he shrugged with one shoulder—"it does."

"Really? It seems so...."

Seth smirked. "Don't tell me you're afraid of needles."

"I wouldn't get that past you, would I?"

"Not a chance." He had, after all, been the one I'd trusted to carve a much more bearable variety of pain into my upper arm.

"Okay, it's not the needles. I just don't get how it's supposed to work."

"I guess it, I don't know, gets the qi moving the right way or... yeah, something like that."

"The qi? Seriously? You of all people buy into that?"

"I don't know if I buy the qi part, but something works."

"I can't believe anyone talked you into even trying it."

"It took him a while, believe me. I've known Michael since before he went to Hokey Pokey school, and he *still* had to twist my arm for two years after I had my car accident." Seth gestured at his neck. "Made all the difference in the world. That shit's amazing."

"So what finally changed your mind? Did he bring you a stack of peer-reviewed studies or what?"

"Honestly?" Seth glanced at his waiting client, then turned to me again. "I was in so fucking much pain after that wreck, and nothing was helping. Michael sat me down and told me he couldn't deal with seeing me like that when he had a shot at helping me. And then he said the worst-case scenario was that it would do nothing, and the best-case scenario was that I'd be able to sleep again."

Sleep. God. *Sleep.*

"All right. Sold." I gestured at Seth's client. "Don't let me keep you from your work. I can get the number when you're done."

"The hell you can." He nodded toward the desk behind the counter. "My cell is next to the computer. It's an awfully technical phone, but I'm sure you—"

"Shut up." I chuckled.

Seth returned to his client and put on a pair of fresh gloves. As the tattoo gun buzzed to life again, I took the phone off Seth's desk and turned it on.

"It's listed as Tucker Springs Acupuncture," he said without looking up from his work.

"Got it." I found the listing and sent it from his phone to mine. "Thanks, man."

"Anytime. Good luck."

Chapter 2

I MADE the call on Monday afternoon, and on Tuesday morning I followed the receptionist's directions across town to a shopping center a couple of blocks from the freeway. Nothing screamed credibility for a medical professional like setting up shop in a strip mall. On the other hand, I knew all too well how difficult it was to find a place with a reasonably affordable lease and some actual visibility. That was why my nightclub lived in an old converted warehouse on the not-so-nice side of the Light District. Glass houses, throwing stones, etc.

Sitting in my car, I took a deep breath and stared at the clinic.

The sign over the windowed storefront read Tucker Springs Acupuncture between a black-and-white yin-yang and another symbol I didn't recognize. Seth had been after me for two years to do this, and middle-of-the-night desperation had finally made me give in, but now I wasn't so sure.

I was here, though. I'd made the appointment and had the cash in my wallet; cash I could ill afford to spend. Aside from money, though, what did I have to lose? It wasn't like that shit was dangerous or anything. I couldn't imagine there were too many side effects to tiny, superficial needles, and I didn't see myself getting addicted.

I stared at the letters and the yin-yang and the tinted windows below them, silently demanding they justify themselves. Offer proof. Offer some reason for me to walk through that shining glass door. When it came to alternative medicine, I was as skeptical as Seth was about life in general. I regarded every treatment as not only snake oil, but the snake itself. At best, quackery. At worst, dangerous. And no matter what, fucking expensive.

But after the last couple of nights, I was desperate.

On the way inside, I stopped to read the sign in the window. It echoed the name and yin-yang overhead and, in a smaller font, listed the various ailments that the acupuncturist claimed to treat.

Infertility.

Drug addiction.

Vision problems.

Asthma.

On and on and on. God, this smacked of a snake oil salesman. *One tincture to treat every ailment under the sun! A miracle cure! Hallelujah! That'll be $79.99, please—cash, check, charge, or firstborn.*

My shoulder throbbed relentlessly, and my head was light from lack of sleep and the second dose of painkillers I'd taken at six fifteen.

Maybe I was just desperate, maybe I was as gullible as the next person, but two words on that lengthy list drew me through the door:

Chronic pain.

The clinic smelled oddly... herbal. Something pungent, vaguely familiar, and slightly burned. Strong enough I couldn't ignore it, but not powerful enough to be nauseating. I could have been mistaken, but I swore I smelled one particular herb that hadn't been legal until fairly recently, at least not without a government-issued license and a compelling reason.

The waiting area wasn't all that different from a doctor's office, though it lacked the sparse, sterile appearance. Framed prints of tranquil landscapes lined the dark green wall between two mahogany bookcases. A plastic milk crate tucked beneath the table held brightly colored plastic toys, and a few well-worn magazines leaned on each other inside a metal magazine rack. Between a Buddha statue and several books on Chinese medicine was a trickling fountain in a clay bowl. Water ran over pebbles and fake jade, and on top stood a tree that resembled a bonsai tree.

"You must be Mr. Davis."

I immediately recognized the singsong voice of the receptionist and turned my head. He was a cute kid, probably a college student. Square-rimmed hipster glasses, stylishly messed-up hair with highlighted tips, and just a *little* flamboyant. I wondered if he was part of the reason Seth came here on a regular basis. This kid was 100 percent his type, right down to the tan that did not happen naturally in Colorado this time of year.

"Yes," I said. "I'm Jason Davis."

He smiled. "Right on time. Dr. Whitman needs you to fill this out as best you can." He gave me a pen and clipboard. "And be totally honest, because…." He waved a hand and sighed dramatically. "He'll get the answer out of you one way or another, so don't try to hide anything."

I laughed. "Is that right?"

"Trust me." The kid had a mischievous sparkle in his eye. "He's one of those people; you might as well tell him what he wants to know. He's kind of like the CIA, minus the car batteries and waterboarding."

"Good to know."

I took the paperwork to the waiting area and sat beside the table with the books and fountain.

The form was about what I'd expect from any medical professional. The usual crap about injuries and ailments. And of course, *Are you currently taking any medications, including over-the-counter?*

I chewed the inside of my cheek, tapping the pen on the form. I'd heard holistic practitioners frowned on modern medicine. Poisonous chemicals and evil pharmaceutical companies or some crap like that. Whatever. The last thing I needed was a lecture on why I shouldn't be taking the pills that often meant the difference between one hour of sleep and three.

But if he was going to get the answer out of me anyway….

I sighed and wrote *OTC anti-inflammatories + doctor-prescribed Percocet for pain*. The man would probably have heart failure when he found out I was sucking down pain pills instead of meditating or drinking purified water blessed by a unicorn. Oh well.

After I'd filled everything out, I handed the form to the receptionist, then returned to my seat. While I waited to be called back, I fixed my gaze on the trickling fountain. There was a heavy sense of hopelessness in the realization that it had come down to this. That I was desperate enough to try anything that had the slightest promise—mythical or otherwise—of relieving my pain.

What if it didn't help? What if nothing did? I was at my wit's end after five years. What would happen in ten, twenty, fifty years if I couldn't find some sort of long-term—even short-term—relief?

"Jason?" The receptionist's voice brought me out of my thoughts. He raised his chin so he could see over the high desk. "Dr. Whitman's still with another patient, but he should be out in a few minutes."

I forced a smile. "No problem."

My stomach fluttered with nerves. As if I didn't have enough to think about, it occurred to me that I hadn't asked Seth about this guy. They'd been good friends for a long time, which said a lot, since Seth didn't trust most people any farther than he could throw them. I could only imagine the banter between these two. Seth the hard-core prove-it-or-it-didn't-happen atheist versus "Dr." Whitman the acupuncturist.

What kind of person went into acupuncture, anyway? What was I dealing with here? A guy who could sell used cars and bullshit? Or a New Age hippie type who bought into this as much as his clients did?

Give him a chance, Jason.

I closed my eyes and released a breath. I would give him a chance. But the proof had damn well better be in the pudding, or I wasn't buying.

Down the hall, a door opened. As footsteps and a male voice approached, I turned my head. An elderly woman appeared first, and when the source of the male voice came into view, I almost choked on my breath.

Apparently *that* was the kind of guy who went into acupuncture. Holy *fuck*.

I couldn't say if I'd been expecting dreadlocks and hemp or glasses and a lab coat, but what I hadn't been expecting was six-foot-plus of *oh my God* with a heaping dose of *please tell me you're single*. He looked like he'd stepped out of a laid-back business meeting: pressed slacks, a plain white shirt with the first button casually left open and the sleeves rolled to his elbows. His hair was almost black, short enough to be neat, and long enough it *just* started to curl. Long enough for a man to get a grip on if—

Jesus, Jason. You *get a grip.*

A thin string of twisted brown leather hung around his neck and disappeared down the V of his shirt, and he had a beaded hemp bracelet on his left wrist, so he wasn't entirely without the signs of a hippie lifestyle. While the acupuncturist and his patient exchanged a few words, I stared. Goddamn, he was hot. He'd taken that old cliché "tall, dark, and handsome" and made it his bitch. Dark-haired, dark-eyed, tall enough I'd have to look up at him, and his perma-smirk hinted at something devious hiding inside that mind of his. And handsome? Good God, yes. The perfect amount of ruggedness roughened his edges, tempering his borderline-pretty-boy look like an invisible leather jacket and sunglasses. If the receptionist was Seth's type, this guy was undeniably mine.

And then he looked right at me. "Mr. Davis?"

I cleared my throat and stood. "Jason."

He extended his hand. "I'm Dr. Whitman, but most people call me Michael."

"All right. I guess I'll call you Michael."

He smiled, which crinkled the corners of his eyes just right to draw my attention, and suddenly nothing was on my brain except *And I thought I was a sucker for* blue *eyes*. Apparently brown eyes did it for me too.

"Follow me."

Don't mind if I do….

Chapter 3

MICHAEL LED me down a hall with four doors on either side and gestured for me to go into the third one on the left. In the center of the room was a table. Not an exam table, though. Closer to a massage table. Black leather, cushioned, complete with the doughnut-shaped cushion on one end so someone could lie facedown.

"Just have a seat for now. We'll go over your history, primary complaints, and all of that before I treat you."

I sat on the table, and Michael took a seat on a small wheeled stool. He scanned the form, stopping abruptly when something apparently caught his eye. "You own Lights Out?"

I nodded. "You're familiar with it?"

"I've heard of it, but I've never been." He smiled, glancing up through his lashes, *almost* shyly. "Can't imagine I'm exactly part of your target demographic."

I laughed. "Not many people in this town are."

We went through the usual rigmarole, as if I was going to a new doctor. Did I drink? Did I smoke? Pain's a four on a good day, eleven on a bad night, seven right now. Blah, blah, blah.

Then he scowled at the page, and I didn't have to ask which part he'd read.

"So you're taking Percocet?" He looked up at me. "How often?"

"Whenever I need it."

He raised an eyebrow. "And how often do you need it?"

I shifted uncomfortably. "A few times a week. Usually when I can't sleep." I paused before quickly adding, "When the pain keeps me up at night, I mean."

"I see." He glanced at my form, then blew out a breath. "And you've been doing this for how long?"

"I'm not addicted to them," I said through my teeth.

Michael patted the air, and his voice was gentle. "I wasn't making any accusations. I'm more concerned about the burden long-term use of a narcotic puts on your liver."

"On... my liver?" I cocked my head.

He nodded, scribbling a few notes on the form. "Kidneys too."

"You're not going to tell me to stop taking them, are you?"

Michael narrowed his eyes slightly, and I suddenly understood the receptionist's comment about car batteries and waterboarding. Michael hadn't said a word, but I was certain he saw right through me, right to the "fuck you" that was ready to light up in red neon letters the second he told me I shouldn't take anything.

He folded his hands on top of the form. "I'm not going to tell you that you can't or shouldn't take them. What I'm hoping to do is remove your reason for having them at all."

Oh God, please.

I swallowed. "And if you can't do that?"

"Then I'm not doing my job." He held my gaze for an uncomfortable moment. "Tell me, how exactly did you injure your shoulder?"

My face burned. Hell if I knew why. Wasn't as if I hadn't told this story to a million people before, usually with embellishments to make sure everyone laughed uproariously at my stupidity, so why did it make me self-conscious now?

I cleared my throat. "I suppose 'showing off like an idiot' isn't a conclusive enough answer?"

Michael laughed. "Not really, but it's certainly an intriguing one." He inclined his head. "Go on."

"I was mountain biking, took a single-track trail way faster than I should have, lost control, and face-planted." I gestured at my shoulder. "Landed on my face and my shoulder."

Michael grimaced. "How is your neck?"

"My neck was fine, thank God. Scraped the shit out of my face, but the helmet protected my head. My shoulder took the brunt of it."

"Better that than a head or neck injury."

"No kidding. Or swallowing my teeth."

He shuddered. "Indeed. Fortunately, I think we can manage the injury you do have." His eyes narrowed again as if he were reading me somehow.

"Something wrong?" I asked.

"You're carrying a *lot* of stress."

I laughed dryly. "Am I getting that gray already?"

"No." A grin flickered across his lips. "But the tension isn't just in the area where you're experiencing pain. You get headaches when you're tense, don't you?"

"Doesn't everyone?"

"Some more than others." He gestured between his eyebrows. "But I'm guessing yours radiate from here?"

This guy was good.

"Sometimes, yeah," I said. "But you know how it is. Stress about money, that kind of shit."

He groaned. "Oh, believe me, I know that feeling very well."

"Really? I figured you'd be raking it in here."

Michael shrugged. "I'm not a cardiologist."

"So you're a peasant like the rest of us?"

"Basically. Anyway, you get that heavy ache in your forehead that makes your eyes hurt, right?"

Shit. He was *really* good.

"Yeah, I do."

"I figured. Next time that happens? Press the sides of your thumbs right here." He demonstrated, putting his thumbs together above the bridge of his nose. "Press in, and then pull them across like so." He pulled his thumbs apart, slowly drawing them along the arches of his eyebrows, and lowered his hands. "Do it three or four times and it should diffuse some of the tension."

"Good to know."

He scanned my paperwork again. "You said you hurt your shoulder five years ago. Aside from the initial healing period, has the pain gotten better or worse since then?"

"It's mostly stayed the same, but…."

His eyebrows rose. "Hmm?"

I shifted, the table creaking quietly under me. "It started getting worse when my relationship went south. And ever since he moved out, I've been struggling financially, so…."

"That'll do it," he said softly. "Stress almost always increases chronic pain."

"Yeah." I laughed bitterly. "And actually, the pain was part of what made my relationship go south."

Michael cocked his head but didn't speak.

I cleared my throat. "My ex, he, uh…. We had some issues, and I think my shoulder turned into an excuse to fight. If I was in too much pain or too drugged out of my head to do much around the house, or I had to cancel some plans, he lost his mind. The way he saw it, I was only in pain when *he* wanted me to do something."

Michael scowled. "And you said the pain got worse when he left? After living under that kind of pressure, I'm surprised it didn't improve."

"He left me with both halves of a mortgage I can't afford." I rolled my shoulders gingerly. "It's nice to not have to justify taking it easy anymore, but…."

"Yeah, I can understand that."

He continued through my history, asking questions about everything from my health to my family to my job. I gave him vague answers about financial issues and the loss of the club's co-owner, neither of which I *ever* liked talking about, and he didn't press for details. Strangely, his line of questioning didn't prompt a "none of your goddamned business" reaction the way it probably would have if I was talking to my doctor or dentist. It helped that he didn't make any snarky comments about "damn, if it weren't for bad luck, you wouldn't have any luck at all." I'd give anyone a free pass to ask away as long as they didn't jump on the "which god did *you* piss off?" bandwagon. I couldn't figure out how some the information he requested was relevant to fixing my damned shoulder, but I answered without hesitation.

Car batteries and waterboarding indeed....

"Usually I'd have you lie down," he said, "but I'm going to have you sit up so I can access points on the front and back of your shoulder. I'll need you to take off your shirt. Shoes and socks too."

I did as he asked while he reached into a small chest of drawers and pulled out a handful of plastic packets. When I looked closer, I realized each packet contained an individually wrapped needle, each resembling a two-inch-long antenna. A little less than half of the needle was thicker than the other with a small loop on the end. They were so fine, I couldn't imagine them breaking through anything—never mind skin—without bending.

As he laid out the needles, he glanced at my upper arm and did a double take. "Wow, that's quite a tattoo. Seth's work?" I almost expected him to run his fingers over it the way some guys did. Kind of hoped he would. Really hoped he would.

I also hoped he was oblivious to the phantom tingling where he, being a professional, *hadn't* run his fingers across my inked skin. "Yeah. Seth did it. He did an amazing job."

"I don't think I've ever seen him do a tattoo that wasn't amazing." He met my eyes and laughed softly.

"So this means you don't have a problem with needles, then?"

"Yeah, something like that." I didn't, but admittedly, my stomach knotted up a little as he tore open one of the packets. "So, um, tell me how this works?"

"The body has energy flowing through it. Qi, as the Chinese call it. Sometimes the channels get blocked, or interrupted, and the needles"—he gestured with the one he'd freed from the package—"help with those blockages. If you'll pardon the pun, the point of acupuncture is to get the qi flowing properly."

In my mind's eye, I saw him digging beneath my skin with the sharp instrument until he'd bent the channel o' qi to his will. I was pretty sure that wasn't how it worked, but the mental image didn't do much to relax me.

Evidently seeing the apprehension written across my face, he said, "Trust me on this." When our eyes met, his half smile—combined with what the low, warm light did to his already-dark-brown eyes—certainly stimulated my heart. Among other things.

But then he took a seat and focused his attention on my foot, and I remembered the needles he hadn't yet put in. He slid the needle into a thin plastic tube, and the hairs on the back of my neck stood on end. As he pressed the tube against my foot just below my ankle, I held my breath.

Then he tapped the end of it and, a second later, slid the tube off, leaving the needle sticking out of my skin at a sharp angle.

It didn't hurt. Well, that wasn't entirely true. It hurt, but not like I'd expected it to. There was the briefest sting, there and gone so quickly I barely noticed it, but the ache that followed was… strange. It was a dull feeling, but almost electric.

I flexed my ankle.

"Doing all right?" Michael asked.

"Yeah. It just feels weird."

"It's different, especially the first time." He leaned down and positioned another needle. He tapped it into place so it was almost perpendicular to my skin, and the same warm, achy sensation with tingling edges bloomed around its point. "What you're feeling is deqi."

I raised an eyebrow. "The what now?"

"Deqi." He looked up from freeing a third needle from the packaging. "The sensation of the qi arriving."

"I see." I watched him slide the needle into the plastic tube. "So is this the kind of thing where I have to be a believer for it to work?"

"It's acupuncture, Jason." He tapped the needle into place. "Not Santa Claus. It'll still work even if you don't believe."

"Good to know."

He switched to my other foot, and curiosity got the best of me.

"Okay, I have to know. My foot? When I'm here for my shoulder?"

He nodded without looking up. "I'm concerned about your liver and kidneys and how they've been affected by the medications you've been taking. So this will stimulate them and help them flush out some of the toxins." He positioned the needle about an inch below the base of my first and second toes, right between the bones.

"Uh…." I studied him. "Isn't… isn't the liver… *not* in my foot?"

"The liver channel begins in the feet. Stimulate and unblock that channel—" He paused to tap the needle into place. "—and it helps to soothe and decongest the liver."

"Soothe? Decongest?" I shook my head. "You're the expert here."

"Trust me on this." He glanced up, and I'll be damned if the son of a bitch didn't wink. "I know what I'm doing."

Somehow I doubt you know all *of what you're doing, Dr. Whitman....*

As he continued, I couldn't decide what was more fascinating: the needles themselves or his long, nimble fingers manipulating them with expert precision. I had no doubt there was a complex technique to all of this, one he'd spent years learning. There had probably been a time when he'd been clumsy and uncertain, but now he made it look easy. Effortless.

After he'd finished putting needles in my feet, he stood. "Okay, now for a few in your shoulders."

"What about these?" I gestured at the ones sticking out of my skin. "How long do you leave them in?"

"Oh, you know. Come back in a week or so."

We locked eyes, keeping straight faces. Then the corner of his mouth twitched, and I laughed.

He chuckled as he turned away to pull out a drawer from the cabinet. "Just ten or fifteen minutes." Something rustled and clattered. "Usually I'd leave you to relax and let them do their job, but I'm thinking your shoulder needs a slightly more... active approach."

"Active? In what—"

He turned around again, and I damn near groaned aloud.

The receptionist just had to mention a car battery, didn't he?

In one hand, Michael held a plastic box about half the size of a phone book. Several knobs stuck up from the top, and one side had about ten places to plug in peripherals. In his other hand, he had half a dozen thin red and black wires. On one end, they had plugs to connect them to the box. The other end? Miniature fucking jumper cables. Of course.

"Do I get a choice between this and waterboarding?"

Michael rolled his eyes. "Nathan loves telling people that."

Regarding the machine warily, I said, "Yeah, but he told me *minus* the car batteries and waterboarding."

"Don't worry. All these do is put a mild electrical current through the needles. Problems like what you're experiencing sometimes need extra stimulation to get the qi flowing properly."

I still wasn't so sure about this thing. "Why do I get the feeling the people who invented acupuncture didn't have those?"

He smirked. "Well, even Eastern medicine has made advancements, you know."

"So has the CIA."

Michael laughed. "Relax." He set the machine on the table beside me and laid the wires on top of it. "The worst you might feel is a dull ache."

"I'll take your word for it."

"If it's too intense, say so, and I'll either turn it down or remove the needle. I don't want you to be in pain."

"Much appreciated."

He rested the heel of his hand on my shoulder, and I took a sharp breath.

"Is that tender?" He lifted his hand away.

"No, you're fine. I just"—*shouldn't like you touching me that way*—"wasn't expecting it."

"Sorry." His hand put his hand back. A second later he pressed the plastic tube against my skin.

I closed my eyes and tried to concentrate on the impending sting and ache. When he tapped the needle, it stung, and it ached, but I was only half-focused on the weird sensations. My tingling nerves were too busy following the warmth of his hand wherever he touched me.

I had never thought I'd be disappointed when a man was finished arranging needles in my flesh, but I was.

He reached for the box and its cables. "I'm attaching the leads to the needles," he explained. "And I'm going to tape them down so they don't yank the needles out."

I shuddered. That was one more mental image I didn't need.

As promised, he taped the leads down. Then he turned on the box, and as he adjusted the currents, he manually tweaked the needles. It felt as if he was... stirring them? Moving them, anyhow, but not in a way that was painful. It reminded me of a dentist doing work while I was numb—I knew he was doing something, and it seemed like it should have hurt, but it didn't. It wasn't even unpleasant, necessarily, just weird.

And he was right about the electric stimulation. A warm, dull ache radiated from the needles, along with an intermittent tingle that sometimes bordered on uncomfortable, but it was only unpleasant inasmuch as it was alien. But even while he manipulated the needles sticking out of my flesh, I couldn't keep my mind off his hands. I swore his fingertips were more electric than the jumper cables.

Jesus Christ, Davis. Get a fucking grip.

It was impossible to guess how long this went on. I closed my eyes and let him do his thing while I savored every time his skin brushed mine.

"Jason?"

My eyes flew open. It was less the sound of my name that startled me, and more the gentle heat of his hand around my upper arm. "Sorry, what?"

"You all right?"

"Yeah, why?"

"Are you getting light-headed?"

"I—" I was a little dizzy, wasn't I?

That's what happens when you forget to breathe, dumb-fuck.

I glanced back at him and smiled. "No, I'm fine."

He eyed me uncertainly, then released my arm— *no, your hand can stay there!*—and went back to work. "If you need to lie down or anything, speak up."

"I'm fine," I said. "Just need to remember to breathe."

Michael laughed. "That's usually a recommended part of the treatment, yes."

I laughed too, which pushed some more air into motion and alleviated the dizziness. "Guess you were relaxing me a little too well."

"That's why I usually have people lie down for this." He steadied my shoulder with one hand— *ah, there it is*—and adjusted a needle below my collarbone. "But I want to work on the front and back simultaneously." He leaned to the side so we could make eye contact. "I can do the front, then back, if lying down would be more comfortable."

"I'm fine. This is fine."

"You're sure?"

I nodded. He held my gaze for a moment, then continued.

Maybe five minutes later, he was finished, and removed the taped leads before coming around to stand in front of me.

"Let me check your pulse." He beckoned, and when I extended my arm palm up, he clasped the back of my hand in his while he pressed his fingers to the inside of my wrist. I had no doubt my pulse was elevated now, and rising.

He didn't comment, though, as he made a note of my pulse. "How does your shoulder feel now?"

"Better, actually." *I'll be damned. It really* does *feel better*. "Still a little stiff, but…."

"Good. There's one more thing I need to do, and this might sound strange, but—"

"Is this the part where you want to see my tongue?"

He laughed. "Seth warned you, eh?"

"Yeah. I thought he was fucking with me."

"Nope. Afraid not. So…." He made a "go on" gesture.

"Do I have to say 'ah'?"

Michael laughed again. "Whatever floats your boat, but I still need to see your tongue."

And I'd like you to do something besides look at it.

Good thing this was a slightly awkward examination. At least if my cheeks were as red as I thought they were, he'd probably write it off as me feeling ridiculous rather than embarrassed by the thoughts wandering through my mind. And maybe a little flustered. Just a little.

Okay, a lot.

"All right," he said, and I closed my mouth as he jotted something on the form.

"Dare I ask what you're looking for on my tongue?"

"You can tell a lot about someone by their tongue," he said so matter-of-factly, I felt like an immature schoolkid for completely misinterpreting the comment.

"Can you, now?"

Michael nodded. "The color and the texture say a lot about what's going on elsewhere."

I cleared my throat. "Really?"

"Mm-hmm," he said. "For example, looking at yours, I definitely need to focus some attention on your liver and kidneys. Probably the gallbladder too. Between your tongue and your wiry pulse—"

"Wiry pulse?"

Another nod. "It's a sign of your liver being out of balance, as well as a secondary deficiency in your kidneys."

"So what do I need to do about that?"

"I'd recommend coming back to see me. Between the acupuncture, some dietary changes, and maybe some herbal treatments, we can get everything back to functioning the way it's supposed to."

I exhaled. "How many times do you think I should come in?"

"It'll probably take at least seven or eight visits to get you back on track. After that? It's up to you if you want to have regular treatment."

I scowled as I mentally calculated the cost. Michael must've encountered this a lot, because he went on, "If money is an issue, especially since insurance doesn't usually cover my treatment, we can work out a plan. I can't give away my services, but if I can help, I'll do what I can to make the treatment accessible."

Tempting. Very tempting. "Thanks. I appreciate it."

He gave me a few of the usual pointers—ice, not heat, dumbass—and then removed the needles from my shoulder and my feet.

I put on my shirt and shoes, and Michael led me out into the hall. On the way back to the waiting area, I had to squint as my eyes readjusted to the fluorescents overhead and the sun coming in through the tinted glass. Why was it so surreal to be out here again? Even my own car, the shopping center, the view of the mountains, seemed… strange. As if I'd been on an altogether different plane for a little while.

We shook hands. Then I turned to finish with the receptionist and Michael took another patient back. As he disappeared down the hall, I debated taking him up on his offer to work out some kind of financial plan.

I just couldn't decide if I wanted to come back for the acupuncture or the acupuncturist.

Chapter 4

FIVE YEARS ago my business partner, Rico, and I had gotten our hands on a deserted factory on the eastern edge of the Light District. After pouring an unholy amount of borrowed money into renovating the place, not to mention getting liquor and the permits to pour it, we'd hung up a sign, lit up the dance floor, and Lights Out was born.

The night we opened, Rico had beamed from behind the bar as our DJ played to a packed house. "Like a phoenix from the ashes."

With the cash flow these days, I was more inclined to compare it to a zombie no one had the heart to shoot in the face.

Tonight the club didn't open until nine, so the lights were on and the chairs were up. Instead of pulsing techno, the room echoed with clinking bottles, running water, chattering voices, and the muted, tinny music coming from the smaller stereo behind the bar.

With the regular lights on, the walls were plain blue, black, and white. Once we turned the black lights on later, dozens of brightly colored designs would appear. Not that people paid any attention to them, considering everyone would be either drunk, flirting, or both, but it made for a cool atmosphere.

As I walked across the club to the staircase, Brenda, one of the bartenders, spoke to me from behind.

"Wow, Davis." When I turned around, her eyes widened. "You get some new drugs or something?"

"Uh, no. Why?"

She shrugged. "I don't know; you just look... different."

"Really?"

Brenda glanced over her shoulder. "Hey, Tony. Come here a second."

Tony sauntered out from behind the bar. "Yes, dearest?"

She nodded sharply toward me. "Does he look different today?"

Tony scrutinized me. "Well, you do look more awake."

"Seriously?" I raised my eyebrows. "Am I usually that bad?"

They both laughed.

"Davis, darling." Tony clicked his tongue and shook his head. "No offense, but you usually look like ass when you show up."

Brenda nodded. "He's got a point."

"Gee, thanks," I said. "You're both quite the flatterers today."

"Hey, I call it like I see it," Brenda said matter-of-factly. "You usually either seem like you're in terrible pain, or you're high as a kite. And today you're…." She gave me a down-up glance and then shrugged again. "I don't know, you just look… better."

I smiled. "Well, let's hope it lasts 'til the end of shift, right?"

"Yeah, no doubt," Tony said. "Don't need you scaring off all the hot boys."

I laughed as I started up the stairs. "If I wanted to scare off all the hot boys, I'd have you get on the bar and dance."

"Hey! I could outdance you, skinny boy!"

I chuckled and kept walking. Upstairs, the dance floor was deserted and quiet, the Tiffany-style lamps over the pool tables dark, and the barstools empty. I didn't see any of my bartenders, but chatter from the back room told me they were here. I trusted them to take care of the prep work before the club opened—if that shit didn't get done now, then they got to slice limes and fill ice bins while ten people waited for drinks. Their funeral.

I left them to it and continued to my office, which was tucked into a converted storage room between the bar and another storage room.

I still hadn't moved Rico's desk out of here. Lately I'd been piling papers on it as an excuse to avoid filing them. Or moving the desk. I didn't have time for the former or the heart for the latter. Maybe someday.

I went to my own desk and sank into the plush leather swivel chair I'd bought myself for my birthday a couple of years ago. Then I stared at my inbox, especially the black binder that had materialized there since yesterday. Apparently the bookkeeper had dropped it off. It took no small amount of mental arm-twisting to convince me to finally reach for it.

Perusing the numbers, I couldn't ignore the sinking feeling in my chest. We weren't just in the red, we were almost to the bone. Tapped out, wrung dry, and overdrawn on favors and loans alike.

If not for my shoulder, I might have laid off a couple of bartenders and handled their shifts myself. It wasn't as if I didn't know their job inside and out, but the aftermath was a guarantee of an excruciating night of hot showers and pill-popping.

The DJs were already stretched thin and underpaid. If I lost any servers or bouncers, the remaining staff would have to work overtime, which I couldn't pay right now. Or I'd have to close one of the two levels of the club, which would piss off my clientele. The college kids liked to get wild on the louder, brighter first floor, while the thirty-and-up crowd preferred the lounge atmosphere of the second. The younger patrons drank gallons of cheap liquor and beer, but plenty of money flowed upstairs, where the bartenders poured wine, microbrews, and top-shelf Scotch. Raising prices might work in the short term, but only if I wanted to lose some clientele, especially those who good-naturedly—for now—ribbed my bartenders about the overpriced booze.

"We'll figure it out," I heard Rico saying a year and a half ago when things weren't nearly this bad. "Don't worry, man. We'll find a way."

I let my gaze slide toward his vacant, paper-stacked desk.

Sure we will, Rico. Sure we will.

And I would. I just needed something to give. A cushion of a few hundred dollars a month, and maybe I could get my head above water. A bill that went down instead of up. Maybe Uncle Sam could back the fuck off instead of swooping in for his piece of the action whenever I almost got ahead.

I rubbed my forehead. Of course, Wes *had* to leave me saddled with this damned mortgage when I was already barely keeping the business going on my own. His credit was already fucked all to hell—what did he care if the bank foreclosed? So when he left me, he stopped contributing to the mortgage. And with the value tanking thanks to the shit real estate market, I couldn't sell without losing my shirt.

My boyfriend was gone. My business partner was gone. My quality of life was shit more often than not. It was only a matter of time before something else fell the fuck apart.

Maybe it was just stupid pride, but I was bound and determined not to close the club, declare bankruptcy, or let go of the house. I sure as hell wasn't doing all three. Fuck admitting defeat.

And now my damned head was throbbing. From right between my eyes, a deep, relentless ache radiated up to my hairline and out to my temples. Resting my elbows on my desk, I dug my thumbs into either side of the bridge of my nose, hoping some counterpressure might alleviate the pain. Or make my head explode, which would solve a few problems.

"Next time that happens?" Michael had said. *"Press the sides of your thumbs right here. Press in, and then pull them across like so. Do it three or four times, and it should diffuse some of the tension."*

I glanced at the closed door. There was no one around to see me, but I still felt like an idiot.

I pressed my thumbs between my eyebrows and moved them apart the way Michael had demonstrated. It didn't kill the headache, but it did relieve a little bit of the pressure, so I closed my eyes and did it again. A third time.

After the fourth time, I lowered my hands and looked at the bills in front of me.

And my head didn't hurt.

I blinked a few times. What the hell?

The ache in and behind my forehead had faded. Significantly. A vague heaviness remained, reminding me that there'd been pain there a moment ago, but the worst was definitely gone.

For that matter, my shoulder still didn't hurt, which was unusual when I was stressed. Cautiously, I rolled my shoulders. The muscles were tight, a bit stiff and achy, but most of the pain was MIA. Stretching carefully, I closed my eyes and smiled to myself as I exhaled.

I was drowning in problems, but if only for a little while, I wasn't in pain. I wasn't. In fucking. *Pain.*

And if only for a little while, I couldn't ask for anything more.

"HEY, HEY, someone's looking better," Seth shouted over the upper level's music. We clasped hands in that handshake that looked like we were about to start arm-wrestling. "How's the shoulder?"

"A lot better." I rolled it as if for emphasis. "That shit's amazing."

He grinned, raising his beer bottle in a mock toast. "Told ya."

"Yeah, yeah, you were right. Come on."

Seth followed me past the bar and down the hall by the restrooms. I pushed open the door marked Employees Only, and we continued up the metal stairwell to the roof where we always went to chill when he came by the club.

More than once, I'd considered opening this as a terrace level for the club, but the liability made me break out in hives. What if a drunk went over the side? What if a cigarette didn't make it into the designated receptacle and the whole place went up? No, no, no. This was, and would be for the foreseeable future, the outdoor break room.

Seth leaned against the railing, idly tapping his beer bottle on the bricks. "So Michael helped, then. Glad to hear it."

"More than I expected, that's for sure." I threw him a pointed look. "You could have warned me he was hot."

Seth laughed. "Well, I didn't want to ruin the surprise." Bringing his beer up to his lips, he added, "Too bad he's straight."

I scowled. "Yeah, I was afraid of that."

"Damned shame he doesn't play for our team. I mean, I thought he did a few times, but…."

"What do you mean?"

"In high school, I'd have sworn he had a thing for this kid who was in the band with us."

"Did he, now?"

Seth nodded. "Michael and I were both first chair trumpet players. He was a super talented, amazing musician back then. Probably still is. Anyway, junior year, this kid Charlie Turner moves to town. I swear, the day Charlie sat next to us, Michael couldn't remember a damned scale." He laughed, his expression taking on a distant look. "I thought for sure Michael was gay after that. Or at least bi. Curious. Something."

"But he isn't?"

"Nope. There wasn't a varsity cheerleader in our school who didn't date him, and I'm pretty sure he banged his way through two sororities in college before he met his wife."

"Damn it, he's married too?"

"*Was* married."

"But still bats for that team."

"As far as I know, yep."

"Bastard."

"You know how it is." He shrugged. "All the good ones are taken or straight."

"Gee, thanks."

He laughed. "Hey, I'm single too, so…."

"Yeah, but we're talking about the good ones."

"Oh, fuck you."

I snickered, then rested my elbow on the concrete railing and faced him. "So, you guys went to high school together? How did you both end up in this godforsaken town?"

"You know my story, but Michael's son has a lot of problems with asthma, that kind of shit. The smog in LA wasn't doing the poor kid any good, so Michael and Daina wanted to move him somewhere with cleaner air." He gestured up at the night sky, which was dotted with stars that even the faint city lights

couldn't dim. "I suggested Tucker Springs, and here
they are."

"You?" I raised an eyebrow. "You who is forever
complaining about being stuck here and how there's
nothing in Tucker Springs? *You* persuaded someone to
move to this town?"

"Okay, so it's boring as fuck and I'd love to leave,
but I could see why someone with a kid would live
here. Especially if it makes a difference with health
problems."

"I suppose that makes up for the dullness,
doesn't it?"

"Apparently. And hey, it means I have my old
friend nearby. Don't see him as much as I'd like, but
it's more than once a year now."

"And the acupuncture's a bonus, right?"

"You'd better believe it."

"Speaking of which, thanks again. I don't know
what the fuck he did, but…."

"Helped, didn't it?"

"God, yes."

"Glad to hear it," he said. "You gonna see him
again?"

"I want to, believe me."

"Money?"

"Always."

"If you need it, I can—"

"No way, Seth." I put up a hand. "I can't let you
pay for this. It's too much."

"And we both know it's too much for you to afford." He pointed at the club beneath our feet. "You've
got this place to leech off your wallet."

"Yeah, and you've got overhead and shit to deal with." I shook my head. "I can't. Thanks, but I can't."

"Well, the offer's there if you need it."

"I appreciate it." And I did, but I couldn't take his money.

No matter how badly I needed to see Michael again.

Chapter 5

I COULDN'T escape daily—even hourly—reminders that I was a financial failure, and few things made me feel more ashamed than being on a first-name basis with the guy at the Light District's biggest pawnshop. Didn't have much choice these days, though, so I pushed open the door, pretending not to notice the place's familiar smells. It was mostly aging vinyl and ammonia-based glass cleaner—a distinctive mixture I could have identified even blindfolded.

The bittersweet smell of failure. I shoved the thought out of my mind as I approached the case at the front of the store.

Emanuel—El to most of us—stepped out from the back and grinned. "Jason! My friend. You coming to bring me money?"

I cringed, trying not to think about the four out-standing items I had in hock. Probably wouldn't see any of that shit again.

"I wish." I ignored the familiar camera beneath the glass case between us. "Coming to get some money, I'm afraid."

"Man, keep it up and I'm gonna have to change that sign to say Jason Davis's Personal Fucking ATM."

"In my dreams, right? Then I wouldn't have to dig through my house every other week to find something to bring in." I set a leather-and-steel watch on the counter, trying not to remember how much I'd coveted the damned thing before I finally bought it. "What can you give me for this?"

He studied me instead of the watch. "You doing all right? You don't look so good."

I scowled. Less than a week after my appointment, and my shoulder had already begun going back to its old ways.

El tilted his head. "You're trying to do something for your shoulder, aren't you?"

My cheeks burned, but there was no point in trying to get the truth past El. He was way too familiar with the problems spanning from my physical health to my financial. "If I can pay for it, yes, it's something new for my shoulder."

He pursed his lips. "Something new?" One eyebrow climbed his forehead, and he drew back a little. "Jason, I'm not gonna judge, but if this is for a drug habit…."

"No, no, it's nothing like that." I shifted my weight. "Acupuncture."

"You? Acupuncture?" El blinked. "Somebody put a gun to your head or what?"

I laughed. "No, Seth talked me into it."

"And it works?"

"So far, so good." I gestured at my shoulder. "Just need another hit."

"Hey, whatever floats your boat, my friend." El smirked. "But if he asks you to take your pants off, you'll know he's planning on sticking more than needles in you."

I chuckled. "I wish, believe me."

"Think that would help the pain?"

"Fuck, I don't care." I grinned, not even a little ashamed of the goose bumps rising along my arms. "You should *see* this guy."

"Is that right?" El thought for a moment. Then he put a hand on the small of his back and winced dramatically. "You know, I think I feel a sudden pain coming on myself."

I laughed. "Yeah, well, before you go get treated for that, I need to see him about my shoulder." Humor fading, I tapped the watch. "Which is why I'm here."

El's lips thinned. "How much do you need?"

"How much can you give me?"

He scowled, locking eyes with me for a moment. Then he shifted his attention to the watch. "It's in good shape, but these things don't sell so good. Thirty-five's the best I can do."

I exhaled. "Shit…."

He drummed his fingers on the glass beside the watch. "Sorry, man. I'm stretching it as it is."

I absently rubbed my neck, trying to knead out the tension that threatened to creep up from my shoulder. But if that ever did a goddamned bit of good, I wouldn't be here trying to score some cash like a jonesing drug addict so I could get a hit of the only thing that *did* help.

El eyed me. "How much do you need?"

I shook my head. "I'm not going to ask you to give me more than it's worth."

His brown eyes bored right into me. They weren't as intense as Michael's, but they were just the right shade to make me think of my acupuncturist's, and there went my knees. I casually leaned against the case, holding El's gaze.

When he spoke, his tone was nonnegotiable. "Jason. How much do you need?"

"I'm not—"

"Let me rephrase that," he said. "How much is the appointment?"

I shifted my attention to the watch to avoid his scrutiny. "It's sixty-five."

"And how much do you have?"

"Not enough." But I knew the answer he was really after. Closing my eyes, I exhaled sharply. Shame tangled in my gut and heat rushed into my face as I muttered, "If I want to eat for the next week? I have about twenty."

El pushed out a sharp breath. "Man, that club is going to suck you dry."

"Yeah, tell me about it. And if the club doesn't kill me, the house will."

He nodded but didn't say anything. We'd had this conversation enough times. Close the club, let go of the house, cut my losses—El probably knew as well as I did that there was no point in discussing it. I'd deal with the long-term cataclysm that was my financial life eventually. Somehow. In the short term, I needed this.

"Sixty-five, then?" he said.

I didn't look at him. "Thanks."

He printed out the usual forms and wrote the pertinent information, then handed them to me. I didn't bother reading them. El would tell me if anything had changed since the last time I was in here, and God knew I'd read these things enough to know them by heart. I just signed on the dotted line and slid the forms across the case. El checked them over, signed them, and put them under the counter.

Then he pressed the bills into my hand. "Well, my friend, I hope the acupuncture keeps helping."

"Thanks." I took out my wallet and slipped the cash into it. "Believe me, I hope it does too."

El and I made small talk for a few minutes, shooting the breeze about our respective businesses, the amazing new microbrews that a pub down the street had recently added, and whether we thought the Broncos would pull it off this year. Then we shook hands, and I left with enough cash in my wallet to pay for one acupuncture appointment.

As I walked into the clinic, Nathan looked up from behind the tall desk, batting a few strands of hair out of his eyes. "Mr. Davis, right?"

I nodded. "Yeah, I hope I'm not too late?"

"Oh, honey." He waved a hand. "Dr. Whitman's so far behind today, you could go get a coffee and read the paper if you wanted to."

"He's behind already?" I glanced at my watch. "It's not even one o'clock."

"His first appointment of the day ran long." Nathan gave an exasperated sigh. "Then the second one did, and the third, and...." Another wave. "It's all downhill from there. Pretty much standard operating procedure for the doc."

I chuckled, pretending I didn't hope my appointment ran a little long. Hey, I couldn't touch the man, but I wasn't opposed to looking at him for a few extra minutes. Or having his hands on me. Or....

I cleared my throat. "I'll just wait, then. I'm in no hurry."

"Lucky you." Nathan smiled. "Half the patients who come through here are on their lunch break or running off to get their kids. They're always in a hurry, but they sure don't mind staying a little longer with the doc."

"I can't blame them," I said. "Well, I don't work until seven tonight. Whenever he's ready for me."

"Shouldn't be too long. He's usually—" Nathan paused, doing a double take at something on his desk. Then his head snapped up. "Oh my God. You seriously *own* Lights Out?"

"I do, yes."

"Oh, I love that place. Question, though." He leaned forward, lowering his voice to a conspiratorial whisper. "That bartender with all the tattoos and the earrings. You know, the one who looks like he just got out of prison?"

"Caden?"

"Is that his name? Anyway, is"—he dropped his voice a little more—"is he single?"

I shook my head. "I'm afraid he's spoken for."

Nathan clicked his tongue. "Damn it. All the good ones are taken."

"Truth, isn't it?"

As a door opened outside my line of sight, a voice in my head added, *And if they're not taken, they're straight.*

A woman came into the lobby, and at the other end of the hall, another door opened, then closed. Michael must have been working with a few people at once.

I took a seat while the woman paid her bill and left. Someone else emerged a while later. About ten minutes after that, a third came down the hall, and Michael was right behind her.

He glanced my way, and maybe I imagined it, but he seemed to tense a little. He smiled, though, and nodded to acknowledge me, turning away before I could be sure if his cheeks had colored.

I shifted in my chair, turning my attention to the bonsai tree on top of the jade fountain in front of me. Wishful thinking, nothing more. The man was a medical professional, and he was straight, no matter how much I wished he was just a little curious and a lot unprofessional.

"Jason?"

I looked up, and as I stood, Michael said, "How is your shoulder feeling?"

"Better. I mean, it was better for a few days after I saw you. The treatment helped. A lot." Aware that I was rambling, I pointed at my shoulder. "But it's been hurting again. Kept me up most of last night."

Michael pursed his lips, eyeing the offending joint as if it might explain why it hadn't done his bidding. Then he gestured down the hall. "Come on back."

I followed him into one of the rooms. Not the same one as last time, but similarly appointed: dim lights, a massage table, a chair, and a few small cabinets and a chest of drawers pushed up against the walls.

"I'm glad to hear your last treatment helped." Michael closed the door behind us, sealing us into the tiny room. Or, rather, sealing out the rest of the world. Oblivious to my steadily rising heart rate, he said, "Was last night better, worse, or about the same as what you were experiencing before?"

"It was—" I stopped abruptly when he picked up my wrist and pressed two fingertips against it. I gulped, forcing myself not to even glance at his hand. "It wasn't as bad as it's been the last few months."

"Mm-hmm. Did you take anything?"

I hoped the room's dim light masked whatever color might have darkened my cheeks just then. "I, um…." What did it matter if I blushed? He had his damned fingers on my pulse. "I took some Percocet."

"Did it help?"

I shrugged with my good shoulder. "As much as it ever does."

"And how much is that?"

"Took the edge off enough to let me get some sleep. Better than spending the whole night digging the corner of a wall into my shoulder."

Michael cocked his head. He released my hand, made a quick note on my chart, and then he said, "Digging a corner into it? What do you mean?"

I wrung my hands in my lap, focusing on them instead of him. "It sounds ridiculous, but sometimes when it hurts really bad, I'll lean against a corner or some molding. Anything sharp, basically. As hard as I can."

"Which makes it hurt more, right?"

I nodded and didn't look up. "Yeah. It hurts like hell. But when I stop—"

"It's a relief when that pain stops, even if the original pain is still there."

Finally I met his eyes. "Yeah. Exactly."

"And of course the original pain is diminished because of the endorphins released."

"I guess. All I know is, there are some nights it's either pills or the wall. Or both."

He set my chart down. "Well, that's why you're here. The plan is to get you off the pills. And the wall."

"Most people would tell you I'm off the wall to begin with."

Michael laughed. "Not much I can do about that part, I'm afraid." He walked past me to the tiny chest of drawers behind the table I sat on.

"Before we get started," I said, "you told me last time it would take several visits to treat this. Is that... still pretty realistic?"

"I wish I could tell you this was an overnight solution, but this is an injury that's had a long time to set in. Fixing it will take a while."

"It's not the time that's the issue." I swallowed, wondering if this was what it felt like to literally swallow my pride. "It's the money."

"Well, we might be able to work something out. As I said before, since insurance doesn't cover acupuncture most of the time, I run into this a lot. We can find a way."

I laughed bitterly. "Yeah, well, I'm not sure how much you can work around it when it's a matter of food or acupuncture."

Michael stepped into my peripheral vision, and when I gazed at him, his eyebrows were up. "You're not foregoing food for this, are you?"

"Not this time. But there's only so much shit I can pawn to pay for it."

"Ouch." He chewed his lower lip, absently tugging the wrapper on one of the needles in his hand.

"Ouch is right." I sighed. "The thing that sucks? A year ago, I almost had everything under control. I was still struggling, but just about had it to the point where I could make ends meet. Then the housing market got worse, and on top of that, like I said before, I lost my business partner and my boyfriend within a few months of each other, which left me with the business and the whole mortgage, and...." I made a frustrated gesture. "Now I'm basically screwed." I paused. "And for some reason I'm telling you my life story. I swear I'm not trying to get sympathy, I'm—"

"Explaining where you're coming from," he said with a nod. "I understand. And I know the feeling, believe me. The cost of living around here is obscene."

"To say the least."

"I'm starting to wonder if everyone's natural state in this area is 'barely getting by.'"

"Even for a doctor?"

"Yep. Honestly, I'd move out of Tucker Springs if I could. Love it here, but it's so damned expensive."

"So why stay?"

"My kid." He thumbed the edge of the file folder in his hands. "His mother and I have joint custody, and it would... complicate things." He paused, his eyes losing focus. Then he shook himself back to life. "Anyway. I'm trying to stick it out. See if the economy gets better, do what I can to bring in more patients. You know how it is."

"Yeah, I do."

"Of course, I have this place too." He gestured around the room. "Overhead and all of that."

I groaned. "God, I know how it goes. As much as I wouldn't wish it on my worst enemy, sometimes it's good to know I'm not the only one."

"Right?" He laughed humorlessly. "And get this. As a bonus, I had to switch my apartment to month-to-month, which is more expensive of course, because I don't know if I'll still be able to afford it in three, six, twelve months."

"Ouch. Well, just be glad you're not stuck with a damned mortgage."

"I am. Every day, believe me, I am." His eyes took on a distant expression. "But I guess we all have our crosses to bear."

"Yeah." I wondered what else he had weighing on his shoulders. "I guess we do."

Our eyes met.

Then Michael cleared his throat and set the file folder on the seat beside the table. "Anyway. Shirt and shoes off, and go ahead and lie back."

"No car battery this time?"

He laughed. "Not yet. You're just going to relax with a few needles for a while, and then I'll have you turn facedown so I can do some electrostimulation along the scapula."

"Shock therapy," I mused. "Can't wait."

Michael just chuckled.

He must have put in more than a dozen needles, and they weren't concentrated on my shoulder. Hands.

Feet. Two in my scalp. Something to do with soothing the liver and fucking with the gallbladder, apparently. I was only half listening as he explained it; his fingers were on me, and no amount of talking or sticking sharp things into my skin could distract me from them. I barely felt the needles. When he'd carefully parted my hair, he'd sent electricity crackling along my nerve endings, and I didn't even care if he saw the goose bumps. As long as I could keep myself from getting visibly turned on, I was good, and somehow I stayed calm in that department.

In fact, I was calmer than I'd been in a long time. Aware of him and of his touch, yes, but... calm. Relaxed. Never thought I'd feel like this while I probably looked like a human pincushion, but after last night, I'd take it.

I was vaguely aware of Michael moving beside me. He stood—apparently he'd been sitting? Hell, I'd lost track—and stepped away from the table.

"Comfortable?" he asked.

"Very." One word, and it took unimaginable effort to enunciate. "Might fall asleep."

"Good. I'll be back in about twenty minutes."

He dimmed the lights until he became a featureless silhouette against the wall. When he opened the door, bright, cool light spilled in from the hallway, illuminating him for a moment before he stepped out. The door clicked shut behind him, and the room turned mostly dark again.

My eyelids were heavy, so I let them slide closed.

I drifted in and out for a while. Half dreaming, half letting my mind wander. At first I tried to stay as still as possible because I couldn't remember where all the needles were, but soon I had no desire to move anyway. I was too comfortable. Too relaxed.

And as I savored this peaceful sleepiness, my mind wandered to everything Michael and I had discussed earlier. Though the very thought of money could easily negate all this relaxation, that didn't happen this time.

I felt a bit less like a goddamned failure when I knew I wasn't the only one struggling. That, or there was just plenty of room in the failboat for all of us.

My eyes flew open. Michael was in the same situation I was. Barely making ends meet, struggling with the cost of living.

What if….

What would a straight guy think of living with a gay man? What did *I* think about living with a jaw-dropping hot guy I couldn't touch? Still, desperate times did have a tendency to warrant desperate measures, and bringing strangers in as roommates qualified as a desperate fucking measure. Moving a guy like Michael into my house might not do much for sexual frustration, but it sure could make the sight of my bank balance sting a little less.

I had the space. The guest room hadn't been used at all since Wes had left. The only overnight visitors we'd ever had were his parents every couple of months, and I barely went into my home office now that I had a laptop. I could easily clear out that room for Michael or his son.

Michael didn't know me from Adam, but he knew Seth. Seth could vouch for both of us, at least enough to convince each other we weren't ax murderers.

Though knowing Seth, he'd find some way to lord the power of his endorsement over us.

A tap on the door brought me back to the present, and Michael stepped into the room. He closed the door behind him and slowly brightened the lights until I could make out his features.

"Feel all right?" he asked.

"*Oh* yeah."

"Good. I still want to do some electrostim, though."

"You and your car battery."

Michael laughed. "You know me."

I wish....

He turned the light a little brighter and carefully removed all the needles. "Go ahead and lie face-down. Sit up slowly, though, and let me know if you get dizzy."

I obeyed, careful not to jar my shoulder, though I realized as I eased myself upright that it didn't hurt much. It ached and was uncomfortably tight, but the worst was definitely gone. I tilted my head to one side, then the other, before I cautiously rolled my shoulder. Yep, tight and aching, but not excruciating.

Then I lay facedown on the table with my head in the doughnut-shaped cushion.

"Is that comfortable?" he asked. "Doesn't aggravate your neck or shoulder?"

"It's fine."

"Just let me know if you need to move around."

A drawer opened and closed, and some plastic crinkled. Needle packets, probably. Then one tore, sounding a lot like a condom wrap—

Don't go there, Jason. Do not *go there.*

As he positioned the first needle, I suppressed a shiver; men this attractive should not work in hands-on professions. No, scratch that. They should. They should be *required* to. In fact—

A needle stung more than I'd expected, and I jumped, cursing through gritted teeth.

"You all right?" he asked.

"Yeah. They don't usually hurt like that."

"If the muscle's especially tender, they can," he said. "How does it feel now?"

"Still aches, but it's not too bad."

"If it gets unbearable, let me know."

"Will do."

As he continued working, I gnawed my lower lip and tried to find the nerve to bring up what I'd thought about while he'd been out of the room. It was easy to say I could deal with someone this attractive living in my house. It was a little more difficult when that someone's hands were on my skin and I had to concentrate this hard on playing it cool.

It dawned on me that the mere suggestion might make things awkward. Oh, to hell with it. If it did, there were other acupuncturists in Tucker Springs. And I probably couldn't afford them either.

"Listen, um, I know this is way out of the blue, but... hear me out."

He said nothing.

I went on. "It sounds like we're both struggling to scrape by, and maybe we could both use some relief in that department."

"Mm-hmm...." He tapped another needle into place.

"Would you be willing to consider a roommate arrangement?"

Michael's hands froze. "You…. Are you serious?"

I nodded as much as I could in this position. "I know it sounds completely crazy, especially since we're practically strangers, but Seth can vouch for both of us."

"True." For a moment he was silent. I wasn't sure if he was mulling over the idea, concentrating on arranging needles, or both. Then, "You do realize I have joint custody of my son, right? So he'd be living with me part of the time?"

I nodded again. The fact that he hadn't shot down the idea gave me a rare inkling of hope.

"And that doesn't bother you?" he asked.

"Why should it?"

His hands halted for a moment, then continued what they were doing.

After a lengthy silence, he said, "It's an interesting thought. I'm not committing either way, but tell you what: Print out a lease agreement. Let's get together outside of the clinic and talk specifics, and…." He tugged gently on a cable, then picked up the machine. "Maybe we can work something out."

Chapter 6

THE FOLLOWING afternoon, I strolled through the Light District with a manila folder tucked under my arm. Nothing was set in stone yet, but the idea of a roommate alleviating some of my financial woes made me feel a hell of a lot better.

In a decent mood for once, I relaxed and enjoyed my scenic surroundings. The Light District was one of those cool mismatched areas with weird shops and eclectic artwork at every turn. It was originally supposed to be a gathering place for authors, poets, musicians, and artists. But apparently it attracted those who thought they were God's gift to the arts but didn't have the chops to crack it, so sometime in the early 1970s, someone in the literature department at Tucker U, the private university at the north end of the city, dubbed the neighborhood Hacktown. The nickname had stuck for a while, though it wasn't used so much anymore, but the artsy patchwork of people and places remained.

Most of the wannabe artists had moved out, and this had become the heart of Tucker Springs's gay community. Hopefully it didn't bother Michael to meet me here. Then again, if he was the least bit homophobic, he and Seth wouldn't be so close, and I doubt he would've considered moving in with me. If wandering through this neighborhood made him break out in hives, this arrangement probably wouldn't work out.

I waited for him at a table in front of one of the brewhouses lining the town square at the southwest corner of the Light District.

I was early, so I lounged with my coffee cup on my knee and the sun warming my back. My wallet and keys sat on top of the manila folder, acting as makeshift paperweights so the gentle breeze didn't scatter the lease agreement all over the pavilion. The weather was unseasonably warm considering spring was still settling in, and there wasn't a cloud in the sky to block my view of the snow-dusted mountains carving a jagged line to the west. It was a spectacular day to go tearing down a one-track trail in the lower elevations. Maybe someday I'd be able to do that again.

Here in town, dozens of people were taking advantage of the weather. A trio of skateboarders with their pants hanging off their asses wove between couples and families, the plastic wheels of their boards clattering across the square's reddish bricks. The bike rental stand must have been making a killing—their expansive rack only had two bikes left. The brewhouses and coffee shops had all opened their patio seating, and even at four thirty in the afternoon, most of the tables were occupied.

Days like this, I could see how Tucker Springs drew people in. I supposed it was an all right place to live. Expensive as fuck, and definitely not for the faint of heart in the wintertime, but it wasn't all that bad. Maybe I was just jaded because of how my life had gone in the past year or so and I was ready to blame whatever was handy. What easier target was there than a quiet little town with a lot of shit that sounded better on paper than it actually was in person? Especially this place.

Take the name of the town itself. If the founders had believed in truth in advertising, they'd have called it Tucker Mud Puddle. The only time the springs were noteworthy was after a major storm or some serious runoff from the mountain snow, at which point the road conditions were so bad they were barely accessible anyway.

And then there was Villa Condominiums, the place my ex and I had lived before we'd bought the house. Condos, my ass. Call them what you want, they were still cramped boxes stacked in among other cramped boxes with a narrow, echoing metal grate stairwell that seemed fine until you tried to move a couch up to the third floor.

Condo or not, the real estate market was god-awful, and we should have known better than to buy a house after we'd barely sold our place without losing our shirts and a few limbs for good measure. But then, the plan hadn't been to buy it and then leave anytime soon. Phrases like "settling down" and "staying here awhile" had been tossed around enough that buying in a shit market had been a hell of an opportunity, not a chance to get fucked up the ass. And not in the way I liked getting fucked up the ass.

But we'd bought the place, and then I'd had to go and get hurt. And that had brought out the worst in Wes. His usual impatience—good God, the man couldn't stand any inconvenience—had been a lot harder to take when it was directed at me. Listening to him swear at a red light or grumble about a delayed flight had been amusing. Catching that "are you ready to go *yet*?" look when something as simple as putting on a shirt nearly brought me to tears? Not so much.

My mood soured, I swallowed the last of my coffee and tossed the cup into a nearby trash can. Then I sat back and thumbed the folder containing the lease agreement while I watched the crowed with unfocused eyes. Maybe things would look up now.

If Michael agreed to move in.

Hell, if he didn't, I could always find a different roommate, but I liked the idea of someone with a mutual friend. And I wasn't opposed to eye candy.

Except I was asking to drive myself insane with him around my house. He was off-limits—straight, my acupuncturist, my roommate—so eye candy was as far as it would go. That didn't mean *other* people couldn't touch him, though. God help me if he brought home any "company" for an evening.

And speak of the devil, there he was. One second the crowd was a blur of faces; the next it was a blur of faces behind Michael as he strolled toward me, sunglasses on and hands in the pockets of his jeans. The sun glinted off his watch, drawing my attention to his arms. His sleeves were rolled to the elbows again, revealing his lightly tanned forearms under a sprinkling of dark hair.

I stood, and we shook hands before we both sat, metal chair legs scraping across cobbles as we inched closer to the small round table between us.

Michael rested his foot on his opposite knee and absently—nervously?—tapped the side of his ankle with his fingers. "So, sharing a place, you really think it's a good idea?"

"You don't?"

He's here, though. That's a good sign.

He shrugged. "Just mulling it over, I guess. It's tempting, I'll give you that. I'm not sure if…."

"Maybe it's a good idea, maybe it isn't." I folded my hands in my lap. "If it doesn't work out, there's nothing saying we have to stick with it forever."

"Except the bit about paying first and last month on a new apartment, deposits, all that shit." He blew out a breath. "This isn't an entirely risk-free proposition."

"Is any proposition?"

"No, I suppose it's not." He was quiet for a moment, then gestured at the file folder beneath my wallet and keys. "That's the lease agreement, I assume?"

I slid it toward him. "It's nothing out of the ordinary. Just a boilerplate agreement I found online. It's all negotiable if there's anything you don't like."

Michael picked it up, and as he perused the pages, I did *not* take advantage of his preoccupation to check him out. Not me. No way. Because when he tilted his head forward to read, he totally wasn't at the perfect angle to make me wonder what the skin of his neck tasted like. Didn't cross my mind at all. Not once.

Jason. Dude. Snap the fuck out of it.

I muffled a cough. "By the way, in the interest of full disclosure, the mortgage payments are twenty-three hundred. For rent, I'm asking for a thousand a month. That'll include everything except food and what not."

"Really?" He cocked his head, inadvertently exposing another fraction of an inch of his neck. "Not fifty-fifty?"

"Not when I'm getting equity on the place and you're not."

"Hmm, good point. But I'm bringing two people in, not just one."

"And he's only there half the time. But I'm not too worried since I have to pay the mortgage either way, and quite honestly, at this point, I need anything I can get to supplement it. Besides, if I ask for any more, it isn't really worth your while, since rent on a two-bedroom is about twelve hundred or so."

"Plus utilities and all." He smiled. "You're offering a pretty appealing arrangement. I don't want to screw you over."

You can screw me over anything you—

"Don't worry about it. You'd be doing me a huge favor paying half that much."

Michael closed the folder. "Well, I do want to see the place before I commit to it."

"Of course." I took out my phone. "Want to make sure you're not moving into a crack house?"

"Pretty much. Though you don't strike me as the type to be running a place like that."

"Looks can be deceiving."

He chuckled. "Not that deceiving."

Our eyes met, and his knowing smile made me shiver. Should've remembered who I was talking to here. The man had probably already guessed what kind of artwork I had on the walls and what shows I TiVoed.

Shifting my attention back to my phone, I tapped the photo album of shots I'd taken earlier today. "Anyway, here are some pictures of the house." I handed him my phone.

He took it and thumbed through the album. "Wow. It's a beautiful place."

"Thanks." I laughed dryly. "Thought I was getting a great deal on it, but...."

He glanced up from the pictures. "Anything wrong with it?"

"No, no, nothing wrong with the house itself. I love the place, actually. But I went into it thinking there'd be two incomes paying the mortgage, and, well, that didn't quite work out."

"Yeah, I can relate," he muttered, and kept thumbing through the album. When he'd finished, he set the phone down and slid it back to me. "I'm definitely interested. Are you sure this isn't an imposition for you, though?"

"Not at all. And for the record, as far as I'm concerned, it's no different than if we'd rented the place together from day one. Yeah, I own the place, but I'm in the same position you are, so I'm not about to lord it over you."

"And you're absolutely sure you don't mind having my son move in too?"

"Of course not."

"Good," he said quietly, possibly more to himself than me. "He'll only be there half the time anyway. His mother and I switch every other Wednesday night."

"How old did you say he is?"

"Seven," Michael said. "And he's a quiet kid. A little on the shy side, but… his mother and I are trying to help him come out of his shell. Point being, he's not the type who'll be running screaming through the house."

I laughed. "Well, that's always a plus. But, I mean, he's a kid." I shrugged. "I have nieces and nephews. I know the drill."

He nodded, glancing at the folder containing the lease agreement. "You know, to be honest, with the position I'm in, I'm half-tempted to sign sight unseen."

"I know the feeling." I looked at my watch. "How much time do you have?"

"I'm free this evening. My son's with his mother, and I've already closed the clinic for the day."

"Why don't we go over there now?"

MICHAEL PARKED beside me in the driveway. As I got out of the car, I glanced around the cul-de-sac. I had a few nosy neighbors who didn't have a lot to do—the kind who still hyperventilated about the fact that *one of them* lived in this respectable neighborhood—and they were probably already speed-dialing each other to announce that I'd brought a man home. Again. In broad daylight, no less, shameless bastard that I was.

I laughed to myself.

I wish, ladies. Believe me, I wish.

I keyed open the front door and led Michael inside. He looked around the entryway. I followed his gaze, taking in my familiar surroundings as though I'd never seen them before.

The floors were hardwood, the kind that creaked with the slightest pressure, and the cavernous rooms amplified every sound. A house this size had seemed like a good idea when Wes and I were talking about things like "forever" and "a family," but living here alone made my skin crawl almost as badly as paying the mortgage on my own.

I shook myself out of my thoughts and led Michael down the hall. On one side, the living room. On the other, the kitchen and barely used dining room.

In the living room, the walls and built-in shelves were conspicuously empty. Not completely, as if I were someone who deplored clutter, but they were occupied by just enough small items—the odd framed photo, a couple of books on the coffee table—to imply there should have been more. And there would have been, except most of what I had beyond furniture and basic electronics were either in Wes's new place on the other side of the country, or in El's pawnshop.

"It's all pretty sparse right now," I said with a self-deprecating laugh. "Sooner or later I'll get around to making it look like someone lives here."

"If a seven-year-old moves in, you probably won't have to worry about that." Michael glanced at me, eyebrows up.

I waved a hand. "Won't be any worse than anything I've done to the place. Be thankful you weren't here when I thought I could retile the kitchen."

"Didn't go so well?"

"Uh, no."

"Did your shoulder have anything to do with that?"

"Well, maybe a little. But mostly I'm just completely inept at home improvement projects."

He laughed. "You too, huh?"

"Not much of a handyman?"

"Definitely not."

"So much for getting free labor out of you," I said with a smirk.

We both chuckled, and I led him into the kitchen. "Nothing in here gets a lot of use, I'm afraid. I'm not much of a handyman, and I'm even less of a cook."

"I *wasn't* much of a cook." He peered around the kitchen. "But the whole single-parenting thing doesn't lend itself to avoiding the kitchen."

"I suppose if someone else is depending on you for food…."

"Exactly. And no kid of mine is subsisting on fried, processed shit."

"Comes with the territory of your job?"

He nodded. "I'd be a hypocrite and a half if I told all my patients to eat right and then parked my son in front of the TV with a plate of fish sticks and a Coke, you know?"

"Yeah, I guess you would be, wouldn't you?" I made a sweeping gesture. "Anyway, use whatever you need in here. But don't drink my Coke or eat my fish sticks."

Michael touched his forehead in a mock salute. "Duly noted."

"Let's see, what else? Oh, the garage. It's big enough for two cars, but I suspect it's going to wind up storing everything that's in the two rooms upstairs."

"My car can sleep on the curb. I'm not worried."

"Mine too. When it gets to be winter, we'll deal with clearing shit out so we can bring the cars in, but this time of year…." I shrugged.

"Perfect."

"The bedrooms are that way." I nodded toward the stairs, and as he started up them, I followed. Totally wasn't an excuse to check out his ass or anything. Totally didn't check out his ass. Or how those jeans fit perfectly, especially when he walked, and—

God. I'm going to live with this guy? He'll be treating me for tennis elbow in a week.

At the top of the stairs, I gathered what wits I had left and cleared my throat.

"The master bedroom is down at that end of the hall." I pointed that way, and then in the opposite direction. "Down here, the guest room and what used to be my office. Both rooms would be yours, and there's a bathroom between them."

Michael checked out the rooms but said nothing.

"Fair warning," I went on, "the acoustics in this house aren't great. I swear to God, I can hear a spider sneeze in the kitchen from up here."

"Could be worse. There's a railroad about three blocks from my current apartment."

"Well, just don't say I didn't warn you. Especially since I get home from work at three or four in the morning sometimes. I try to be quiet, but…."

He waved a hand. "Don't worry about it. I can sleep through anything, and so can Dylan."

"Good to know."

I opened the door to the room formerly known as my office. It still had a desk and a few file cabinets, plus the three-year-old computer that was woefully obsolete. Some framed family photos gathered dust on the walls alongside my degree and a few snapshots from various camping trips.

Across the hall was the sparsely furnished guest room. Nothing but a bed, dresser, and a couple of nightstands, though the wall above the queen-sized bed still had the faint rectangular shadow where a painting had hung for a couple of years. I knew we shouldn't have used that cheap-shit paint, but "I told you so" was bitter, cold comfort when you only found out how badly the paint had faded because your boy-friend was taking pictures off the walls and leaving.

Tearing my gaze away from the evidence of Wes's departure, I gestured at the furniture. "I can move all of this out to the garage or down to the basement."

"With some help, I hope?" Michael shot me a pointed look.

"Yes, of course. You didn't think I'd try moving it all myself, did you?"

One eyebrow rose.

Christ, he really is *good.*

I cleared my throat and broke eye contact. "I, um, can get some help."

"Good," he said with a sharp nod. "Otherwise I'm going to use the dull, rusty needles to treat your shoulder afterward."

"All right, all right, I won't pick anything up, I swear."

"That's right, you won't." He threw me what was probably supposed to be a glare of sorts, but then we both laughed.

I continued showing him around and eventually took him out to the back deck.

"Wow." He rested his hands on the railing and scanned the yard. "Dylan will *love* this."

"Outdoor kind of kid?"

"God, yes." He smiled fondly. "Between his step-dad taking him skiing and me taking him hiking, it's a wonder he hasn't run away to live in the woods."

I chuckled. "You're a hiker, then?"

He nodded. "Which makes living here a definite plus." He gestured at the mountains. "It'll probably take me fifty years to hike all the trails out there."

"You ain't kiddin'," I said. "I've lived here my whole life, and I'm still checking them off my list. You been up to the springs yet?"

"Not yet."

"Don't bother."

"Really?"

"Yeah. Trust me. You're better off going down to Colorado Springs and dealing with the tourists." I paused. "I mean, it's a nice hike up to Tucker Springs, I'll give you that, but don't expect much when you get to the end."

Michael shrugged. "As long as it's a nice hike."

"Oh, it's a beautiful hike. I prefer the more technical ones, but it's a nice walk through the woods."

"Technical ones are the best kind. Not a big fan of the ones that involve serious climbing, though."

"Yeah, tell me about it."

He glanced at me, eyes darting toward my shoulder, and grimaced. "Yeah, I guess rock-climbing isn't very high on your list these days, is it?"

"Well, that's why I'm going to you, right?" I grinned. "So I can climb Horton Peak by the end of the summer?"

"Good luck with that," he said dryly. "I'm not a miracle worker."

"What?" I sighed dramatically. "Seth is a fucking liar, then."

We exchanged glances and chuckled again.

Then Michael cleared his throat and turned around, looking up at the house. "So, the rent. You said it's a grand a month. All-inclusive."

"Yes."

"Seems like a steal now that I've seen it in person. Are you absolutely sure you don't want me paying half?"

"It's fine. A thousand a month and we're good."

"All right, well, I have to give my landlord thirty days. The earliest I could move in is the first of May, so if you can wait a few weeks…."

"That's fine. As long as there's a light at the end of this tunnel, you won't hear me bitching."

"Great." Smiling, he extended his hand. "You've got a deal."

Chapter 7

WHEN I showed up at Michael's clinic for my next appointment, a little boy was sitting behind the reception desk with Nathan. He couldn't have been older than seven or so, and he was unmistakably Michael's son. If I'd seen a picture of the boy, I'd have sworn I was looking at Michael in his youth. Same brown eyes, same dark hair that wanted to curl, and when he got older and lost some of the roundness in his face, he'd probably have the same sharp features.

Nathan greeted me, but he and the boy quickly shifted their attention to something on the computer monitor.

"Oh, follow that guy." Nathan pointed at the screen. "He'll take you to the wizard so you can level up."

I leaned on the desk. "Does Dr. Whitman know you're slacking off?"

"Slacking off?" Nathan gestured dismissively. "Please. I'm teaching his kid to play *Trollquest*. That's not slacking." He put a hand on the boy's shoulder. "Right, Dylan? What are we doing?"

Without looking up, Dylan said, "We're pwning newbs."

I arched an eyebrow. "And you're getting paid for this."

Nathan shrugged. "It's a tough job, but somebody's gotta do it."

"Uh-huh."

A moment later Michael emerged from one of the rooms at the end of the hall. "Oh, hey, Jason." He smiled. "I see you've met my son."

"Well, sort of." I laughed. "He's a little busy."

"Still?" Michael rested a hand on the back of the boy's chair and scrutinized the screen. "You're already at the ice caves? How did you get past the trolls at the gate?"

Dylan snorted. "The gate trolls are easy."

Michael scowled, glaring at Nathan.

Nathan batted his eyes. "What? Not my fault you can't aim."

Shaking his head, Michael looked at me, his lip quirked like "can you believe these two?"

I just chuckled.

Michael squeezed his son's shoulder. "Pause it for just a second. I want you to meet Jason."

Dylan clicked a button and pulled his gaze away from the screen and shifted it up to me.

"This is Jason," Michael said. "He owns the house we're moving into next month."

The kid drew back a little, eyeing me shyly.

"Go on." Michael nudged his arm. "Remember what Mom said?"

Dylan hesitated but then extended his hand. "It's nice to meet you."

I gently shook his hand. "Nice to meet you too."

As he let go, he asked, "Do you play *Trollquest*?"

"I played it when it first came out." I craned my neck to see the screen. "Back before the graphics were *that* good."

"My dad plays." Dylan glanced up at Michael. "He tries to."

"Hey!"

Nathan smothered a laugh.

Michael threw him another playful glare. "You really are a bad influence on my kid."

"Hey." Nathan showed his palms. "You want me to keep an eye on him? You take whatever I teach him."

"Great." Michael groaned, then gestured at me. "Come on, let's go back so they can finish their quest in peace."

"*Finally*," Nathan said with mock exasperation.

Dylan giggled, and I followed Michael down the hall.

"He's a little shy," Michael said as we stepped into one of the rooms. "He'll warm up to you, though."

I shrugged. "It's all right. My sister's kid is shy too. Don't worry about it."

Michael met my gaze. "And you're really okay with him staying at the house? Even part-time?"

"Why wouldn't I be?"

"Uh, well. A first grader moving into your bachelor pad?"

I laughed. "If it was a one-bedroom apartment, it might be an issue. Honestly, you're bailing me out of a shit situation. I'm not going to complain about your kid living with us too."

He studied me, then relaxed. "All right. As long as you're really sure about it. This is getting me out of a bad situation, but I don't want to take advantage of you."

You can take advantage of me all you—

I cleared my throat and broke eye contact. "Don't worry about it. Seriously. He seems like a pretty chill kid, and even if he wasn't...." I met Michael's gaze again. "There isn't much stress a little boy could bring into that house that even remotely compares to what you're offsetting as my roommate. It's cool. Trust me."

He released a breath. "Okay. Good. First part of May still work for you?"

"The sooner the better."

"Perfect. Now let's have a look at that shoulder."

ABOUT A week before the end of Michael's last month in his apartment, he backed a U-Haul into my driveway. We'd both recruited a small army of friends to help move him in, and every inch of the cul-de-sac's curb had a car parked in front of it. Later in the day, I'd fire up the grill and pay everyone with steak and beer, but for now, there was work to do.

I reached for a box, but Michael caught my arm.

"Don't even think about it."

Though my shoulder had been feeling pretty good lately, I didn't argue. Putting up my hands, I said, "I'll, um, supervise."

He smiled, and I pretended goose bumps weren't working their way up my back.

"Excellent," Michael said. "Someone needs to keep an eye on all this riffraff."

"Hey!" Seth's voice turned both our heads. "I heard that."

"Speak of the devil," Michael said with a grin.

"Yeah, whatever." Seth flipped him off. "Fuck you."

Along with everyone else we'd brought over, Seth and Michael got to work unloading boxes and furniture while I stood back and tried to find some way to be useful. Even though Michael's treatment had made a huge difference, my shoulder was still far from healed. There wasn't much I could do today unless I wanted to be in agony later. So, I supervised. At least I had the decency to refrain from lounging in a lawn chair with a beer and sunglasses, though it was tempting, if only to mess with Seth.

I glanced around the cul-de-sac. Curtains had moved aside, faces peered out windows, and I could only imagine the frantic gossiping going on as boxes and furniture made their way out of the truck. Edna and Kristine stood on their respective sides of the waist-high fence between their properties, eyes as big as saucers while they talked behind their hands. Someone was moving in, that was for sure, but *who*? You would've thought the simple U-Haul in the driveway was a rainbow beacon of glittering gayness invading their quiet suburban neighborhood. Not that I was surprised. They'd all watched intently when a similar truck had come to collect Wes and his belongings. I'd been endlessly amused at the reactions—running the gamut from relieved to openly disappointed—when people found out I still lived here. Chuckling over them was better than agonizing over Wes being gone.

I turned away from the gawking neighbors and watched a couple of the guys moving a small bed frame down the ramp. Dylan's, I assumed.

Seth came out of the house and paused to wipe his sweaty brow with the back of his hand. "So did you guys deliberately schedule this on the hottest day of the year?"

"Hottest day?" I scoffed. "Please. We're barely out of winter. Be glad we didn't wait until August."

"I'm surprised you didn't," Seth muttered. "Just to be dicks."

"We thought about it." Michael clapped his shoulder. "Picked a hot day to make you miserable, Wheeler." He grinned. "Mission accomplished, yes?"

"Yeah, yeah. Fuck you, Doc." Seth glared at him suspiciously. "This is a ploy to get me back into your office, isn't it?"

"Of course," Michael said with a flippant shrug.

"And all of this so you can live with that yo-yo." Seth pointed his thumb at me. "You have any idea what you're getting into?"

Michael laughed. "I think I'll manage."

"Keep telling yourself that." Seth turned to me. "You going to help carry anything, or what?"

"Nope." I put up my hands. "Doctor's orders."

"It's true," Michael said. "He picks anything up that weighs more than ten pounds, there'll be hell to pay."

Seth snorted. "Well, shit. I want to see the 'hell to pay' part, so Jason, why don't you—"

"You paying for his acupuncture?" Michael threw him a pointed look.

"Uh, no." Seth turned to me. "On second thought, why don't you take it easy?"

"Planning on it." I grinned. "As for you, how about less jawing, more picking shit up and carrying it?"

Seth grumbled something about heat and slave labor. Then he peeled off his sweaty T-shirt and draped it over the porch railing. With a groan, he clasped his fingers over his head and stretched.

And I'll be damned if Michael didn't do a fucking double take.

I mean, I couldn't blame him. Seth and I were friends and would never be more than that, but the man was *smoking* hot. The intricate tattoos covering his arms, most of his chest, and about three-quarters of his back created the perfect excuse to stare at his lean, nearly hairless body. Low-slung jeans over hips that narrow could drive any man out of his mind, so how could I blame Michael for sneaking a glance?

Aside from the fact that he was, you know, *straight.*

Maybe he hadn't seen Seth's more recent tattoos. The elaborate ink work spanning Seth's shoulders and extending down the center of his back was all fairly new. Michael had known Seth for years. It was possible he simply hadn't seen him shirtless in a while.

Then again, Seth was one of Michael's patients. Surely he'd have seen the tattoos by now? More than once?

As Seth disappeared into the U-Haul, Michael's eyes flicked toward me, and in the same instant I realized I'd been staring at Michael, he probably realized he'd been busted staring at Seth. He shook himself and turned away, color rushing into his cheeks.

"Hey, Mike!" Seth called from inside the van. "Give me a hand with this thing."

Michael exhaled, undoubtedly as relieved as I was for the diversion, and disappeared into the van. The metal box muffled their voices and movement, but in my mind's eye, I still saw Michael's double take.

I had to have imagined it, right? Michael was straight. And just because he'd looked didn't mean he'd, like, *looked*. Except he totally did. I fucking *saw* him.

Didn't I?

Wishful thinking, man. Wishful thinking.

Shaking my head, I went into the house to see if anyone needed any help in there.

It only took a couple of hours to unload the truck. Then Michael and Seth left with the U-Haul to get everything else out of the old place. Michael said it was all boxed and ready to go, just needed to be loaded up and taken to his storage unit, so he and Seth could handle it.

While they were gone, the rest of us hauled the remaining boxes and furniture to their respective rooms. Without Michael to keep an eye on me, I carried a few things. Nothing too heavy, but enough to make me feel useful. Though I wasn't sure how wise it was to set myself up to be sore later when I lived with the damned acupuncturist who'd told me to take it easy in the first place.

By two thirty, everything was where it belonged, furniture had been assembled, and all that remained was to unpack the boxes. Michael and Dylan would handle that part on their own.

Out in the backyard, everyone dived into the cooler of beer while I fired up the barbecue. The charcoal had just hit the perfect temperature and I was laying burgers and steaks on the grill when Seth and Michael returned.

"You allowed to drink beer in your line of work?" I asked as Michael dug one out of the cooler.

He laughed. "Don't tell any of my other patients, all right?"

"As long as you don't tell my acupuncturist."

"Not a word."

Michael had just managed to take a seat and crack open his beer when his phone beeped. He glanced at the screen, then jumped out of his chair. "My kid is here. I'll be right back." He set his drink and plate on the plastic table beside his chair and then disappeared into the house.

A moment later he returned, flanked by a petite brunette with a pigtailed toddler on her hip, a sandy-blond guy who was even taller than Michael, and Dylan.

"This is Daina," Michael said. "Her husband, Lee. Their daughter, Amanda. And"—Michael beamed—"of course you've already met my son."

I shook hands with Michael's ex-wife and her husband.

Daina handed Amanda off to Lee, then shifted her attention to her son. "You have something to ask Jason, don't you?"

Dylan shrank back against his mom.

"Go on." Daina nudged her son gently. "You've met him, honey. You know he doesn't bite."

I squatted so we were more or less eye level, and he drew back a little more. "Hey, buddy. Remember me?"

He nodded. Then he glanced up at his mother, and when she gave him a smile, he looked at me and shyly said, "Can I use my PlayStation on your TV?"

"Of course," I said. "Just means we'll have to make some room between the Wii and the Xbox."

His eyes lit up. "You have an Xbox? Can I play it?"

"As long as your folks are okay with that." I glanced at Michael and Daina, and they both nodded. To Dylan, I said, "We'll get it all hooked up tonight, okay?"

"Cool!" He grinned at his mom, who laughed and tousled his hair.

"Daina!" Seth's voice turned our heads, and he approached with his arms out and a beer in his hand. "I haven't seen you in forever."

"Seth!" she squealed, throwing her arms around him. "Long time, no see."

He hugged her tight. "And just *why* haven't I seen you in ages, woman? Hmm?"

"I guess I haven't been slumming in a while."

"Oh. *Oh*." He let her go and put a hand over his heart. "Cut me, I bleed."

She elbowed him playfully. "Builds character."

"Uh-huh." Seth turned to Lee. "So when are you going to come by and have me finish that design?"

"When you'll do the work for free."

"Free?" Seth snorted. "I don't work for free." He didn't need to shoot me a "keep your mouth shut" glance, but he did anyway. I kept my mouth shut. Discretion was the one condition attached to my free ink.

As everyone continued chatting, the doorbell rang. When I opened the door, I wasn't terribly surprised to find Edna standing on the porch.

"I saw someone was moving in." She gestured toward the front yard where the U-Haul had announced Michael's arrival. "Of course everyone wants to say hello and welcome them to the neighborhood."

"Sure, come on back."

At least it was Edna. She was pushing eighty-five, and while she obviously wasn't sure what to make of two men living together the way Wes and I had, she was always friendly. She wasn't outwardly homophobic—all this gay business, as she called it, simply didn't compute.

In the backyard, we approached Michael, who was shooting the breeze with Seth.

"Michael," I said, "this is Edna Morton. She lives two houses down. Edna, Michael Whitman. My new roommate."

"Your—" Edna looked up at me, her thick glasses magnifying her wide eyes. "Roommate?"

"Yes. Just my roommate. He's moving in along with his son."

I struggled to keep a straight face as her eyes widened a little more. To Michael, she said, "You have a son?"

This time it was Michael who fought to hide his amusement. "Yes, I do. I think he's getting some food with his mother, so let me go find him."

She watched him go, then turned to me. "Well, he seems like a nice gentleman. Is he new in town?"

"No, I don't think so. You'd have to ask him."

"And he's… living here…."

Does. Not. Compute.

"You know how it is. The economy and all of that."

"Ooh, yes," she said with a slow nod. "I most certainly do."

A moment later Michael returned with his arm around Dylan's shoulders. "Dylan, this is Edna. She's one of our neighbors."

"Hi," the boy said.

"Hi, Dylan." Edna smiled. "And how old are you?"

Dylan shyly said, "Seven."

"Seven, huh?" She smiled. "Well, my grandsons will be visiting from Michigan this summer. They're right about your age, so maybe you can play with them. Would you like that?"

Dylan nodded but didn't say anything. I don't think he quite knew what to make of her.

I know the feeling, kid.

The rest of the neighbors trickled over to meet Michael, and everyone seemed to think he was all right. They all adored Dylan too. Kristine was more than "all right" with Michael. She'd been visibly uncomfortable with Wes and me but could still put a coherent sentence together. With Michael, she blushed like crazy and it took her three tries to spit out her own name.

Once again, I know the feeling....

Eventually, the backyard barbecue wound down, and around the time the sun set, only the three of us were left. It was amazingly quiet once everyone had gone except for Michael, Dylan, and myself. Sure, every sound from floorboard creaks to muffled coughs echoed throughout the house, but at least it was just us now. The calm after the party.

Michael left Dylan upstairs to unpack his things, and came down to the kitchen. He pulled a beer out of the refrigerator.

"I really appreciate all of this, by the way." Michael leaned against the kitchen counter. "Letting us move in."

"Hey, I need it as badly as you do."

"Win-win, then." He set his beer aside and dug a teakettle out of one of the boxes stacked on the floor. "Fair warning, this shit doesn't smell great."

"Tea? It usually smells pretty good, doesn't it?"

"Usually, yes." He took out a Ziploc bag filled with leaves and twigs, and as he emptied it into the kettle, he continued, "But trust me on this. Some people aren't crazy about the way these herbs smell."

"Dare I ask what they are?" I asked as he filled the kettle with water.

He said something that I could never in a million years have repeated.

"I… beg your pardon?"

He set the kettle on the burner. "It's a bunch of Chinese herbs. And enjoy not knowing what they are or how they taste because I'll probably make you take some eventually."

"Oh good. Can't wait." I sipped my beer.

Tea? I think I'd rather drink hot dog water.

While the kettle warmed up, Michael reached for his beer.

"So you mix tea and beer?" I wrinkled my nose. "Lovely."

He laughed. "Hey, I feel like having a beer. And that"—he nodded toward the kettle—"won't be ready to drink for a bit anyway. So between now and then

I'll—" He stopped suddenly, and his eyes lost focus as he craned his neck as if he was listening for something.

"What's wrong?"

"Damn it." He set his beer down and pushed himself away from the counter. "Dylan's coughing." Now that he mentioned it, I heard it too. A deep, hacking cough that sounded like it hurt. Michael started toward the stairs and threw over his shoulder, "His asthma's kicking up again. I'll be right back."

Moments later Dylan came down the stairs. His eyes were red, and he paused to cough into his elbow.

"Hey, champ," I said. "Not feeling so great?"

He shook his head and coughed again. When he took a breath, he wheezed faintly, so I didn't push him to speak.

His dad came down the stairs behind him with a box under his arm. He nudged Dylan. "Set up your game, kiddo. You're not going to be moving for a while."

Dylan took off his T-shirt and tossed it over the back of the couch. Well, Michael hadn't said anything about folding it or putting it in a hamper. I didn't mind.

The PlayStation wasn't set up yet, but Dylan had a small handheld device. He lay on his stomach on the living room floor and played contentedly, his inhaler within reach, while Michael knelt beside him and started pulling things out of the box: a long, slim pair of tongs. Some cotton balls. Rubbing alcohol. A lighter. Four round glass jars that resembled fish bowls and were about the size of my fist.

Once everything was laid out, Michael picked up the tongs and pinched a cotton ball between them. He dipped the cotton in the rubbing alcohol, and my eyes darted toward the lighter beside the jars.

I cleared my throat. "So, um, what exactly—"

"Cupping. Helps with asthma, especially when his inhaler isn't cutting it." Michael flicked the lighter and held it to the cotton ball. "Ready, kid?"

"Yep." Lying in front of him, idly kicking back and forth the way kids often did, Dylan focused on his game.

Holding the tongs in one hand, Michael took one of the jars in the other. He held both close to his son's back, turning the jar open side down. He put the flaming cotton ball inside it, held it there for a moment, and then pulled it out the instant before he put the jar on Dylan's back, right below his left shoulder. When the jar met Dylan's skin, his shoulder dipped slightly as if Michael had pushed down hard, but the kid didn't wince or make a sound. When Michael released it, the jar remained in place on Dylan's back.

He was about to put a second one in place, but Dylan started coughing again. Michael waited until it had passed, and then, "You all right?"

"I'm good."

Michael put a total of four jars—cups?—on his son's back, then sat cross-legged beside him. After a few minutes, he glanced up at me and must have seen my "what the fuck?" expression, because he said, "Simply put? The suction helps with circulation, stimulating lymph nodes, getting rid of toxins. That kind of thing."

"Which helps with asthma?"

He gestured at Dylan, then put his hand to his ear and raised his eyebrows. It was then I realized the boy's wheezing had quieted.

"I'll take that as a yes," I said.

Michael smiled, ruffling his son's hair. "He's been doing pretty well lately, but I'm guessing the move aggravated his asthma. Stress and all of that. Probably why his inhaler wasn't doing enough this time." To Dylan, he said, "Feeling better?"

The kid didn't look up from his game. "Yep." He paused to clear his throat. "Thanks, Dad."

Michael let the cups sit on Dylan's back for a few more minutes, and then he carefully removed them. Four reddish-purple bruises remained on Dylan's skin, but he didn't seem uncomfortable, and Michael wasn't concerned. Dylan grabbed his inhaler off the floor and his shirt off the couch, and trotted up the stairs with his video game. He didn't cough once.

"Guess it does work," I said.

"You'd better believe it does." Michael stood, and as he carried the cups into the kitchen, he added, "He's done a lot better since we moved to Colorado anyway."

I followed him into the kitchen. "Really?"

"Oh yeah." Michael set the cups on the counter, then pulled a tea mug out of a box. "The pollution and shit in Los Angeles was horrible on his lungs."

I wrinkled my nose, nodding toward the teakettle, which had been heating this entire time and was starting to emit some vaguely bitter odors. "And that god-awful smell doesn't bother him?"

"He's not fond of the taste, but no, the smell doesn't bother him."

"You make him drink that shit?"

"Mixed with enough honey and stuff so he can't really taste the worst of it," he said. "I actually like it, but…."

I shuddered.

"Anyway," he said, "the pollution wasn't doing Dylan any good, so my ex-wife and I decided to move somewhere cleaner. And cheaper, for that matter."

I lifted my eyebrows. "Cheaper?"

"Compared to LA, hell yeah. But it's a little less manageable with one income than two."

"I know the feeling." I glanced at my watch. "Damn it, it's already six o'clock? I guess I'd better get going."

Michael smirked. "You don't mind leaving us here unsupervised?"

I chuckled. "Might as well get used to it, right?"

"Good point."

"By the way, the club's open late tonight and to-morrow," I said. "I'll be getting in around three thirty, four in the morning. So if you hear someone coming in during the night, it's probably me."

"Good to know." He poured his tea through a strainer, then set the kettle aside and looked at me. "Like I said, you won't wake me up."

"Must be nice."

"Shoulder?"

I nodded.

"Don't worry." He winked. "Let me keep work-ing on it, and we'll get to the point where it doesn't keep you awake at night."

"I'm holding you to that."

"I would expect no less." He paused to put his empty beer bottle into the recycling bin. "That is, after all, what I get paid to do."

"Good thing you moved in, then," I said. "Means I might be able to keep paying you to do it."

He smiled. "Well, maybe now, with this arrangement, things will get easier for both of us."

I returned the smile. "Yeah. Maybe they will."

Chapter 8

MICHAEL HADN'T lived with me *quite* long enough to make a dent in my cash flow problems yet, so almost two weeks into our arrangement, the club's books were as depressing as ever. Rising prices. Floundering income. And of course everyone from the bouncers to the bartenders wanted raises, since the area's swelling cost of living affected them too.

Closing my eyes, I leaned back and rubbed my neck with both hands. The earliest twinges were creeping up the left side of my spine, slithering over my shoulder like kudzu and leaving knotted muscles in their wake.

I had to get out of here or I'd stress myself into excruciating pain. Fortunately it was a Tuesday night, so I was the only person in the building anyway. The club was closed Monday through Wednesday, but I usually came in at least two of those days to take care of administrative bullshit.

Fuck it. I'd deal with this tomorrow.

I left the binder open on my desk and pushed my chair back. Closing up the bar on nights like this was a breeze: no food to put away, no cleaning to be done. Nothing but a few lights to turn off, a quick check to make sure doors were locked and cash was in the safe, and I was out of there.

As soon as I was outside, I stopped and took a deep breath. The air was vaguely musty from the near-by river, but clean and fresh. The sun had just sunk behind the mountains, staining the sky a deep red and purple against the jagged silhouette. Beautiful night. Definitely not one to waste on paperwork.

Better to waste it parked in front of the TV.

By the time I was halfway home, I was relaxed enough that I probably could have gone back and tak-en care of all the shit still festering on my desk. But not tonight. For once, I wasn't going to wind myself into knots over paperwork.

Let me have this one night, I begged the universe, *without being in pain.*

About two blocks away from my cul-de-sac, it occurred to me that going home might not be much more relaxing than being at work. Not as depressing, maybe, but now there was stress on both ends of my commute. When I'd suggested that Michael move in with me, I'd known it would be torture to look but not touch. However, three things about this arrangement had failed to cross my mind:

One, the bizarre varieties of healthy food, most of which were some unidentifiable form of plant life, materializing in my refrigerator between my beer and cold cuts.

Two, how incredibly fucking difficult it was to curtail my swearing—especially while playing a video game—because there was a seven-year-old in the room.

And third, that while Michael dressed business casual outside of the house, he reverted back to more casual and less business at home. For Michael, that meant jeans. Nothing else. Just jeans.

Oh God.

We were only two weeks into this arrangement, and I was already losing my mind. I kept telling myself that sooner or later I'd get used to him. Hopefully before he came to the conclusion that I was naturally clumsy. Prone to tripping over my own feet, dropping things, fucking up a video game that I was completely *owning* right up until the moment Michael waltzed in through the sliding glass door with his sunglasses in his mouth and a sheen of sweat from cutting the grass.

Oh well. Losing my mind or not, I finally had some hope of getting my finances back in order. So what if that meant torturing myself with eye candy that sent my heart racing every time he leaned down to get something out of a cabinet? I might go completely insane before all was said and done, but at least I might not go bankrupt.

When I got home, I found Michael in the living room, and he was the polar opposite of me: shirt off, bare feet propped on an ottoman, totally relaxed except for his thumbs on the video game controller.

He looked up. "You're home early."

"Decided to take it easy for an evening."

Nodding, he turned his attention back to the screen. "You could probably use a night to relax. Good for the shoulder."

"If my boss gets pissed, do I get a doctor's note?"

Michael laughed. "Absolutely."

"Awesome. Be right there." I stepped into the kitchen, dropped my keys on the counter, and grabbed a beer from the fridge. After I'd opened the bottle, I went back into the living room.

I glanced at the screen and did a double take. "You know, you are the *last* person in the world I'd expect to see playing *Grand Theft Auto*."

Michael laughed again but didn't look up from the animated sports car eluding police through the streets of Los Angeles. "Don't tell my kid, all right?"

"Secret's safe with me." I eased myself onto the couch beside him. "Didn't think you'd be into something so violent."

"Well, I could do without the part about shooting cops and hookers, but there is something fun about driving around and stealing shit." He glanced at me. "Therapeutic after a long week."

"It's good for that, isn't it?"

"Yep. As long as Dylan isn't here. I can only get this or *Assassin's Creed* out when he's at his mom's."

"You don't let him play this?"

"Fuck, no." The stolen car on the screen crashed into the back of a police car and then plowed over a pedestrian. "He can play this game and watch violent movies when he's old enough to be horrified by them."

"Says the man who just ran someone over with a stolen car."

He steered around a tight corner as he eluded police, and then shrugged. "Hey, I'll have you know I *am* duly horrified." Michael clicked his tongue. "I should have gotten a fuckload more points for that."

I laughed. "You were robbed."

"I was! Seriously." As he kept playing, oblivious to the way his forearms rippled with the rapid movements of his thumbs, or how oblivious I *wasn't* to that effect, he said, "My kid would have a fit if he knew I played this when I don't let him."

"Not until he's old enough to beat you?"

"Oh, fuck that. Never mind. He's never playing it."

"Good call," I said. "You know, my cousin let her kid play this until she found out about some of the sexual content."

"Oh for Christ's sake." Michael gave an exasperated sigh. "If you're going to shelter your kid, at least be consistent about it."

"No kidding. I couldn't believe she didn't mind the violence and crime, but the minute there's anything suggestive…."

"Sounds like something my ex-mother-in-law would do," he muttered.

"Is that right?"

Rolling his eyes, he nodded. "My folks are conservative, but Daina's?" Michael whistled, shaking his head. "Fuckin' A. I mean, they still freak out that I'm going to raise my son as a Buddhist who shuns modern medicine."

"Are you?"

"I wasn't planning to, but if it'll piss off Daina's mom, I'm tempted."

I snickered. "Sometimes it's worth going to those lengths to piss off an in-law."

"Been there?" He glanced at me again.

"Well, not technically an in-law, but I dated a guy whose mother hated my guts. So I kind of milked it and antagonized her a bit."

His lips quirked. "I'm sure your ex loved that."

"He stopped trying to convince us to get along," I said with a shrug.

Michael laughed. "Shit, my ex-wife still pushes her mom and me to get along. Not gonna happen, I'm afraid."

"Can't blame her for trying, right?"

"I suppose not." He paused the game and reached for a mug on the end table.

"Wait, wait, wait." I put up a hand. "You don't drink *tea* while playing *Grand Theft Auto*. What the hell is wrong with you?"

Michael choked on the tea in question but managed to recover before he spit any of it out. "Very funny." He set the mug aside. "I didn't realize there were drink requirements with this game."

"Well, the two don't exactly go together, you know?" I gestured with my beer bottle. "*GTA*'s a beer game, not a"—I wrinkled my nose—"*tea* game."

"Would it make a difference if I said there was weed in the tea?"

I blinked. "You... what?"

He chuckled. "Kidding." He shifted in his seat, and I realized he had four needles sticking out of his ankle and foot.

"Bringing your work home with you?"

"More like bringing home a damned sore ankle." He furrowed his brow as he messed with the needles.

"It's not... weird? Working on yourself?" I asked. "I mean, I guess it's no worse than someone giving themselves injections, but...."

"It's actually a little easier sometimes because I know exactly where it hurts. And it isn't as if I haven't practiced on myself before. Hell, when I was in school, I practiced on anyone I could get my hands on."

Lucky bastards. I wasn't sure if I envied them the free acupuncture or the "hands on" part more. On second thought, if he was still learning at that point, maybe I'd have passed on the needles. "You know, it took a lot of arm-twisting to let you put these in me in the first place. I don't think I could handle being a practice pincushion."

"My ex-wife felt the same way, believe me." He tweaked one of the needles in his foot. "She changed her tune when she found out acupuncture helps morning sickness."

"Does it?"

Nodding, he leaned back against the couch. He gingerly flexed his ankle a few times, then let it rest on the ottoman. "It helps a lot, and she was pretty sick for months. I think she spent almost her entire pregnancy with at least a couple of needles in her skin." He picked up his game controller. "When she was pregnant with her daughter, she kept joking about having me move in so I could treat her on demand." He grimaced. "Lee didn't find that too funny."

"Big shock." I brought my beer up to my lips. "So what possessed you to become an acupuncturist, anyway? I'm pretty sure I never saw that career listed in my guidance counselor's office."

Michael glanced at me, the corner of his mouth raised in a faint smirk. "And you saw listings for gay nightclub owner?"

I laughed. "Touché."

He shifted his attention back to his game and chuckled. "Okay, to answer your question, I'd fucked up my ankle, and a friend pretty much dragged me by the scruff—or the crutch, at least—into her acupuncturist's office. And damn if the woman didn't help with my ankle *and* my migraines and allergies." He slid a pillow under his foot. "So while I was lying there in her office after my fifth or sixth appointment, I decided it was my calling. And here I am."

"Playing video games with needles sticking out of your foot."

"Pretty much."

"So what happened? To your foot, I mean?"

"I was in college, playing basketball with some buddies. Sprained the unholy *fuck* out of my ankle. Still gives me grief sometimes, so—" He gestured with his controller at the foot in question. Continuing his game, he said, "And hey, it's the whole reason I went into acupuncture, so I can't complain too much."

"Guess there are worse ways fate could have gotten your attention."

"No kidding. My mom is convinced it was divine intervention. I think anything capable of divine intervention could have found a less painful means of conveying a message, but what do I know?"

"Better than a head injury, right?"

He laughed. "Okay, good point."

"You said you were already in college when it happened?"

Michael nodded.

"What were you studying?"

"Besides basketball and beer drinking?"

"Dude, we all studied beer drinking."

"True. I was flailing around in college to—oh, motherfucker." He groaned as Game Over flashed on the screen. Then he held up the controller. "Want to give it a go?"

"Hell yeah," I said as I took it. "I'm always good for stealing and destroying a few things to relax."

"Be my guest." He took his tea and sat back while I started a new game. "Anyway, as I was saying, I'd been kind of flailing around in college, trying to figure out what I wanted to do. Thought about premed, thought about nursing. Even looked into an osteopathic college. Then... the ankle incident. What about you?" His mug made a dull, heavy *thunk* as he set it on the end table. "What made you decide to open a club?"

"Delusions of grandeur and the insane idea I could get rich by thirty."

"Ah, the American dream. Open a business, sit on an ever-growing pile of cash."

"More like an ever-growing pile of stress and bull-shit and an ever-deepening pit of debt," I grumbled.

Michael raised his mug. "Well, here's to finding a way to get ourselves out of that pit."

I paused my game and clinked my beer bottle against the mug. As I took a drink, I decided there were definitely worse things than having an attractive straight man around the house, and being up to my ass in debt was one of them.

Yes, this was going to work out *quite* nicely.

Chapter 9

THREE WEEKS after Michael had moved in, I woke up in agony.

It hadn't been this bad in a while, but tonight? Holy shit. One stressful shift at the club and now my shoulder was a glowing ember of pure, unrelenting pain. By the time I couldn't take any more and got out of bed, it had spread into my neck and down the center of my back.

Fuck the shower, I was going straight for the drugs. Moving as slowly as I could, as much for stealth as to keep from jarring my back and shoulder, I went downstairs.

I threw the hot pack in the microwave, and while that warmed up, I pulled a couple slices of bread from the half-gone loaf on top of the refrigerator.

After I'd thrown back a pain pill, I rested one hand on the counter and just breathed while my other hand held the hot pack in place. The pill would kick in sooner or later.

Tensing up will only make it worse, I reminded myself. Slowly, gingerly, balancing the hot pack on my shoulder, I clasped my hands together and stretched my arms in front of me. I breathed deeply, trying to relax.

No luck, though. Minute after minute, the spasms spread out like a growing spiderweb. I couldn't lift my left arm at all, and even raising my right ignited eye-watering twinges.

My gaze slid toward the pill bottle. The only thing that made me hesitate to take two was the threat of more nausea. They wouldn't do me any good if I couldn't keep them down. One pill hadn't helped. Two might finish me off in the sick-to-my-stomach department.

My eyes flicked from the pill bottle to the corner of the wall and back.

I picked the wall.

Holding my breath, I leaned against the corner, pressing back *hard* to dig the sharp edge of the wall into the muscle. Tears stung my eyes, plaster bit into my bare skin, and the darkness behind my eyelids turned red.

When I couldn't take another second, I pushed myself off the corner. Eyes closed, I grabbed the counter for balance as the pain receded, relief weakening my knees and lightening my head. The dizziness didn't help with the nausea, and I held my breath, clenching my jaw and ordering myself not to be sick; I would not be sick, I would *not* be sick.

The spinning gradually slowed, and the queasiness retreated. I let my head fall back against the wall and took slow, deep breaths, savoring the diminished pain. The relief wouldn't last long, but it was all I had.

Too soon, the pain started closing back in, so I pressed up against the wall again. After the third time, the relief was tremendous, but the resulting wave of nausea almost sent me sprinting for the sink. I leaned against the wall, this time for support, and breathed.

Footsteps turned my head, and when Michael came around the corner, he jumped, as if he hadn't expected me to be there. "Oh." He blinked. "I… thought Dylan was up."

I laughed self-consciously. "No, just me. Sorry if I woke you."

"Don't worry about it."

That was when I realized he'd shifted his attention to my shoulder, which I'd been rubbing gingerly. His eyes flicked toward the corner. To the open pill bottle on the counter. Back to me.

Dropping both my gaze and my hand, I cleared my throat. "I, um…." I muffled another cough.

"How bad is it?"

"I'll be fine."

"That wasn't what I asked." He inclined his head. "I can help you, you know."

"Much as I'd love to take you up on that, I'm still fucking broke. There's no way I can pay you until—"

"Jason, you're obviously in pain. I'm not going to let you spend the whole night in this state because of money." He threw me a pointed look. "I'm not asking. Lie on your stomach on the couch. I'll be right back."

He turned to go. As the stairs creaked under his feet, I was tempted to call after him and tell him I was fine, but to hell with it. I felt like shit, Michael was already awake, and he could actually do something more effective than jamming wall corners into knotted muscles.

So I went into the living room as ordered. Fortunately I didn't have a shirt on, because I didn't see myself going through the motions required to take one off. I lay on the couch on my stomach and rested my forehead on my right forearm. I couldn't raise my left arm so kept it against my side.

Michael came into the living room and pulled the ottoman up next to the couch. He sat on it, and at the edge of my peripheral vision, a wrapper tore. Just like before, the sound made me think of a different kind of wrapper tearing, but I didn't let that thought linger.

Dream on, Jason.

Hell, even if I'd had a shot at Michael, it was out of the question tonight with him or anyone else. No way when I hurt this bad.

His hand warmed between my shoulder blades, and I nearly arched into him like a cat, searching for the relief I knew was coming. His touch had become synonymous with both unrelieved arousal and *very* relieved pain, and I only cared about one of those tonight.

The plastic tube touched my skin, and I closed my eyes.

Michael tapped the needle. It stung briefly, the pain gone before I'd really noticed it. Same with the second and third. A fourth, not far from the base of my neck, went in without incident, but from that pinpoint sting, a warm, dull ache slowly radiated. I tilted my head to stretch my neck, pulling at the aggravated muscle.

"Is that painful?" he asked.

"Aches."

"Give it a minute. Tell me if it gets worse."

It didn't get worse. It didn't go away completely, but it wasn't bad. A little annoying if anything. And after the night I'd had, a little annoying was hardly the end of the world.

He gathered up the wrappers and dropped them into the wastebasket next to the couch before returning to the ottoman. "Mind if I ask about something? Just... out of curiosity?"

I rested my chin on my arm. "Go ahead."

"Why are you running the club on your own? You said you had a business partner but don't any longer. What happened there?"

I took a breath, closing my eyes as renewed tension crept into neck and shoulder. "Rico pretty much handled the financial side while I dealt with the marketing, running the actual club, things like that. We had some cash flow problems, but we'd been working on finding ways to get ourselves back in the black. I thought we were doing okay at that point. Money was coming in, overhead was under control."

"What happened?"

"He didn't show up at the club one night." I swallowed the lump that tried to rise in my throat. "I found him in his garage. You know, I always thought that was something Hollywood made up, but no, there he was. Slumped over the wheel of his car with the engine still running."

"My God," Michael breathed. "I'm sorry to hear it."

I sighed. "Rico fucking loved that car. He always joked about being buried in it. I guess when he realized he was going to lose it and everything else, he decided it was a fitting place for, um…."

"Jesus."

I took a breath. "I found out after he died that he'd been taking out all kinds of loans. Used his house as collateral, his car, anything he could get his hands on, and poured that money into the club. From the sound of it, he realized he'd dug himself into too deep of a hole to dig himself out."

Michael was quiet for a moment. "I guess that answers my other question, then."

"What other question?"

He hesitated. "With as much as the club takes out of you, between stressing you out and draining your finances—"

"Why haven't I closed it?"

"Yeah. I'm guessing I know why now?"

"Yes and no." I sighed. "It's partly pride. We both put a lot of work into getting Lights Out off the ground. I'm too stubborn to give up on it until there's absolutely no hope." I paused. "And, yeah, Rico's part of it too."

Michael's warm fingertips met my skin, probably adjusting one of the needles. A faint ache radiated from where he made contact, so that must have been it. When he lifted his hand away, he spoke again.

"It's probably not my place to suggest anything one way or the other," he said, his tone gentle, "but I think he'd understand if you did. If you closed the club, I mean. I can't imagine he'd want you to struggle so hard to keep it going that your quality of life went out the window."

"No, I suppose he wouldn't." I sighed. "Maybe if things get worse, I'll consider it." I turned my head enough to look at him. "But hey, maybe the cash flow will get better one of these days."

He smiled. "Believe me, my business and I are banking on that too." He stood slowly. "I'm going to leave these in for a little while. Try to relax, all right?"

"Will do."

He left the room, and I closed my eyes. I was sure I wouldn't be able to relax, not when I'd been in so much pain—*hey, it doesn't hurt as much now*—and thinking about Rico's death. But the longer I lay there, the more the tension melted out of my whole body, and the more the pain dissipated, fading from glowing red to dull gray. Still there, still unpleasant, but no longer something that made leaning against a sharp corner seem like a rational solution.

Some time passed. A few minutes? Ten? Twenty. Fuck if I knew.

Movement next to the couch dragged me out of the half asleep state I'd slipped into.

"How do you feel?" Michael's voice was low and soothing.

"Better," I murmured.

"Good." He rested his hand on my shoulder, and the warmth of his skin against mine drew a contented sigh from me. "They're probably ready to come out, then." He removed a needle, then dabbed the spot gently with a cloth.

"Bleeding?"

"A little." He dabbed it again before setting the cloth aside. "Happens occasionally."

Apparently that was the only one. He removed the rest without incident and then held my arm gently, steadying me—and unsteadying me, but he didn't need to know that—as I sat up. The room listed, and when I was fully upright, I rested my elbows on my knees and rubbed my temples as I took a few slow breaths.

I cautiously tilted my head to each side and rolled my shoulders. "Oh man. That feels *so* much better."

"Hopefully that'll let you sleep."

"I'm sure it will."

"If you're in any pain tomorrow, let me know."

"Will do." I smiled as I met his eyes. "And thank you."

"Anytime."

We both stood. He started to head for the stairs but hesitated, turning back toward me. "You, um, didn't mind me asking about... you know...."

"Rico?"

He nodded.

"No, it's okay," I said. "Probably doesn't hurt to talk about it once in a while."

"No, I suppose it doesn't." He shifted his weight. "But I didn't want to pry into anything too personal, you know?"

"Don't worry about it."

"All right," he said. "Well, if ever I do step on a nerve, say so."

"I will," I said.

We exchanged tired smiles, and then he continued up the stairs.

I stood in the living room for a moment, just enjoying the fact that I didn't hurt so badly now. The only really annoying part was the burning strip where the corner of the wall must have bitten into my back. There would be a bruise tomorrow, possibly some raw skin that I'd forget about until I got into the shower, but the excruciating muscle spasms had relaxed.

I went back upstairs and slept like the dead.

Chapter 10

THE FOLLOWING day I slept well into the middle of the afternoon, as I often did after the weekend chaos at the club. Then it was errands, a couple of beers with Seth at one of the bars down the road from his tattoo shop, and home well after dark.

I pulled a bottle of water out of the refrigerator and was headed upstairs to relax for a while, but when I walked past the slider, I did a double take.

Michael was out on the deck, barefoot and shirtless—and fucking *hot*—as always. He was oblivious to me, his forearms resting on the railing and his head tilted upward as if he was watching the stars.

I thought about leaving him to his thoughts, but... I couldn't help myself. Something tugged at me, nudging me toward the sliding glass door.

That would be lust, Jason. And some serious wishful thinking.

Probably. Oh well.

I went to the slider, and when I opened it, he glanced over his shoulder.

"Mind if I join you?" I asked.

There was just enough light to illuminate his smile. "Not at all."

I shut the door behind me and strolled across the deck. Folding my arms on the railing, I leaned over it and held my water bottle between my hands.

"You've got a gorgeous view out here," he said, his voice low as if he thought he might scare away all the stars if he spoke too loudly.

"You should see it in the wintertime." I kept my voice quiet too. "Come out here after a good snow when there's a full moon, and it's spectacular."

"Minus the part where it's wintertime in Colorado, right?" he said.

I laughed, and somehow, God knew how, I resisted the urge to stare at him, focusing my gaze on Orion's Belt instead of Michael's. "I didn't say to come out here without a shirt on."

"What fun is that? Shirts are overrated."

On you, they certainly are.

"Yeah, okay," I said. "We'll see what tune you're singing when it's freezing cold and snowing."

He shrugged. "Guess I'll have to stay indoors, then."

Which means I'll have to come out here to cool off.

He turned his head. "How's your shoulder?"

"Not too bad for once." I smiled. "Which I guess I can thank you for."

"Anytime. And hey, if gets as bad as it did the other night, don't hesitate to wake me up."

I sipped my water and set the bottle on the railing. "I appreciate the offer, but I doubt I'd ever actually pester you in the middle of the night unless the house was on fire."

"Well, the offer's open. Better that than spending the night bruising the hell out of yourself with a sharp corner."

Heat rushed into my cheeks. "I suppose that's true."

"If it's any consolation, you're not the only one who does it."

"I'm not?"

He shook his head. "A lot of my chronic pain patients do things like that. Someone described it to me once as banging your head against a brick wall because it feels so good when you stop."

"Put it that way," I muttered, "it sounds even more ridiculous."

"Not really, if you think about it. When you're in that much pain, you'll take anything you can get, even if it only gives you that momentary illusion of relief."

"That sounds about right. At least I'm not crazy."

"I didn't say that."

We both laughed.

"Seriously, though," I said. "Sometimes that seems like the lesser of two evils."

"Better than painkillers?"

I nodded. "You would not believe how many nights I've stood in my kitchen having a staring contest with a bottle of pills. I really, really don't want to take them, and I'm scared to death of getting hooked on them, but sometimes...."

"I can understand that."

"You can?" I eyed him in the darkness. "I figured you'd be vehemently opposed to any kind of drugs."

"I am." He glanced at me before turning his attention toward the mountains again. "Yes, my training tells me that painkillers do more damage than good, but with the pain you've been in for the last five years, I can't exactly begrudge you taking whatever relief you can find."

"Good," I said with a smirk, "because I'd probably have to tell you to go fuck yourself if you did."

He laughed. "Understood. But hopefully you won't need all that shit anymore."

"Here's hoping."

We both fell silent for a few minutes before Michael said, "So how long have you lived here?"

"The house? Or Tucker Springs?"

"Both, now that you mention it."

"I've lived in Tucker Springs all my life," I said. "Well, I was born in Montana, but my parents moved here when I was three, so I've been here as long as I can remember. As for the house, I've had it for a few years now. My ex and I bought it a little while after the economy went tits up. Got a great deal on it." I sighed. "Just didn't think I'd be paying it on my own."

"Best-laid plans," Michael said.

"Exactly." I absently reached up to rub my shoulder, which wasn't hurting yet, but the night was still young. "Even without Wes, I probably could have done fine on my own if not for the club. Whenever the business is in the red, the money has to come from somewhere. If I can't get a loan, it comes out of my profits. And if I'm not profiting, well, it comes out of my pocket."

"I know the feeling," Michael muttered. "Every time I think I'm getting ahead, something new comes up. If I can get out of my student loans, I'll be in better shape, but with minimum payments? Not happening anytime soon."

"God, no shit. I just paid mine off about two years ago. If I still had those, I'd be royally fucked now."

"They're good for that. So why didn't you sell the house? Seems like it'd be better for your stress level if you were out from under the place."

"I keep thinking it might be easier to sell it, but the value is in the toilet, so it'd be a short sale, which takes for-fucking-ever to process, assuming it even goes through. That, and I'd have to force the sale without my ex's signature, which means coming up with—on my own—enough to cover all the nickel-and-diming they do when you're trying to sell a house."

"I can imagine." He glanced at me. "How does that work, anyway? Splitting up with someone when you're not married but own a house together?"

"How does it work?" I laughed dryly. "It's a pain in the ass, believe me."

"Did you buy him out, or what?"

I shook my head. "He'd just as soon let the house go into foreclosure. He already let the bank repo his car, and his credit's trashed, so he has no reason to try to keep up with the mortgage."

"Any way to remove his name?"

"Besides forcing a sale? If I can get his approval, I can refinance it, but I highly doubt the bank's going to approve me for anything like that. Not without a cosigner whose credit is way better than mine."

"Think he'd sign off on it?"

"If I could get ahold of him, maybe." I sighed, shaking my head. "But he won't return my calls, emails, any of that. He's pretty much done with me."

Michael was quiet for a long moment. "If you don't mind my asking," he said softly, "what happened with you two?"

I didn't answer right away. My mind wandered back to the night Wes had called time on our relationship. It amazed me how something like that could still hurt even months after the fact. If he walked through my front door, I'd show him right back out, but the way things ended still stung.

I took a breath. "Wes thought I was a workaholic. Especially after I lost... after the club became my sole responsibility. And, I mean, he was probably right. I neglected the shit out of our relationship because I was trying to keep my business from going under. And trying not to keel over from being in pain all the time." Bitterness seeped into my voice as I said, "So he found someone who didn't have chronic pain but *did* have enough money that neither of them have to work at all, never mind long hours."

"Ouch."

"Yeah."

He glanced at me, grimacing sympathetically. "I can relate to the workaholic thing. That's what my ex-wife thought about me too."

"She thought it?" I asked. "Or you are one?"

"Maybe a little of both. I *was* throwing myself into my work, spending way too long at the clinic every day—like, *every* day—instead of spending time with her." He sighed. "She thought I was obsessed with my work and didn't care about our marriage.

Truthfully, I was throwing myself into my work to *avoid* our marriage."

"Really?"

He nodded slowly, gazing out at the dark mountains. "In hindsight, I was a jerk to her, and I know that. At the time, I was just afraid to face her and all the reasons we hadn't been getting along." He laughed humorlessly, shaking his head. "Guess it was easier to avoid our problems, even if that made things exponentially worse."

"God, I know how that goes. Making your own hours is convenient for avoiding relationship issues, isn't it?"

"Very." He looked up at the sky again. "So how long has it been? Since you and your ex split, I mean?"

"Six months. Seems longer sometimes, though."

"Miss him?"

"Not really." I paused. "Okay, that sounded a bit bitchier than it should have. Sometimes, yes, but most of the time?" I brought my water bottle up. "It's just as well he's gone."

Michael released an amused huff of breath. "I know how that goes."

"Things didn't end so well with your ex-wife?"

"Oh, it wasn't that bad. We get along all right, all things considered. But... we'd been disconnected for so long, and neither of us was ever really sure why. Still aren't. So I'd say the divorce was long overdue."

"Seems like most breakups are."

We both laughed dryly and then fell silent. The stars and mountains alternately gave me something to focus on, but my mind concentrated solely on Michael. I swore my left side, the side closest to him, tingled, while the right was cool from the empty air beside me. Three weeks living together, and I still couldn't keep my blood pressure in check when I was around him.

"My folks called earlier today," he said out of the blue. "You know, checking in, wanting to talk to Dylan." He drummed his fingers on the railing, and that was when I realized his casual posture had changed to that of a man wound up and bordering on agitated.

"Oh?" I said. "How, um... how did that go?"

"It was interesting," he said, more to himself than to me. "They weren't too sure about me moving their grandson in with 'some man.'"

I swallowed. "Because they don't know me? Or because I'm...."

"I didn't tell them you're gay." His fingers tapped even more rapidly. "They, um, assumed you were. Because I'm living with you."

My heart stopped. "I beg your pardon?"

He kept his eyes fixed on the mountains. "My folks are convinced I'm gay."

Good thing I wasn't taking a drink right then or I'd have choked on it. "Seriously?"

Michael nodded.

"What gave them that idea?"

"I guess they...." He paused, shifting uncomfortably. Nervousness and Michael were such a bizarre combination, two incongruous things that shouldn't have existed on the same plane, and yet here they were.

He took a deep breath and pressed his hands down on the railing like he needed its support to stay upright. "Seth's parents and mine were really close when we were kids, and *his* folks, for whatever reason, were convinced I was gay. One day it was the way I dressed, the next it was the music I listened to or the fact that I'd gone camping with three other guys from school. If I dated a girl, she was a beard. Daina was a fucking beard as far as they were concerned." He rolled his eyes. "They were obsessed with the idea."

"Why did they even care? You're not their son."

"No, but I was 'influencing' their son. I think they were in deep denial about him but saw the writing on the wall, so they projected it onto me so I could be the gay one, not him. That or they thought it was catching and assumed I had it, so they were worried about me being around him."

"Even though you hadn't given them any reason to believe you were actually gay."

"That's how scared his parents were of something or someone turning him gay." Michael swore softly. "You know, a lot of people thought it was poetic justice that parents like his wound up with a gay kid. I just think it's fucked-up that Seth got stuck with jerks like them for parents."

"You're not kidding." I'd never met the assholes, but Seth's parents were two of the very, very few people on my "please die in a goddamned fire" list.

"So, his parents were suspicious of any guy Seth hung out with who wasn't a linebacker giving off enough testosterone to be visible to the naked eye." He exhaled. "And since he hung out with me more than anyone and I wasn't so great at the whole macho thing…."

"So it was because of Seth and his parents?" I asked. "Yours didn't…. You weren't…."

He faced me. "Did I give them a reason to think I was gay?"

"Basically, yeah."

Michael gave a quiet laugh. "Let's just say after my dad caught me in my bedroom with the head cheerleader when I was seventeen, he mostly let it go." His laughter faded. "Well, okay, he let it go for a week or two."

"So they still ask?"

He nodded. "Sometimes. They'd spent *so long* hearing Seth's parents question everything I did or said, even catching me with a girl wasn't enough to convince them. I swear, when I told them Daina and I were divorcing, my mother was *sure* it was because I was gay."

I gulped. "You mind if I ask something personal?"

"Go for it."

I hesitated but finally asked, "You *are* just into women, aren't you?"

"Absolutely," he said quickly, almost sharply, but then laughed again. "The head cheerleader isn't convincing enough?"

"Some guys go both ways."

Michael stiffened slightly. "Do you think I do?"

"I don't know. I'm just curious." I cleared my throat. "Obviously it's none of my business. Just, you know, like I said, curiosity."

Michael stared out at the dark yard, something unreadable tightening his expression. "I've never really gotten an answer out of them. If there was something specific about me, I mean. At least they never sent me to one of those camps."

We both shuddered.

"Was that ever suggested?"

"A few times," he said through his teeth. "My parents were even less comfortable with those places than they were with the idea of me being gay, though, thank God. But they never stopped second-guessing me. Even now, whenever I ask them why they thought I was, they sort of pause and give me an uncomfortable 'just wondering' and change the subject." He turned toward me. "When did you figure out you were?"

I played with the cap on my water bottle. "When I was twelve."

"That young?"

I nodded. "Yep. Well, I didn't completely understand what it *meant* to be gay. All I knew was that when one of my friends swiped a *Playboy* from his dad and showed it to us, it didn't do nearly as much for me as the boy band posters my sister had wallpapering her room." The memory made me laugh. Michael laughed too, but it was a forced, uncomfortable sound.

I went on, "Anyway, I was sixteen when I figured out I was gay and what that meant. Came out when I was seventeen, never looked back."

Michael said nothing.

A question crossed my mind, and it wasn't until a second too late that I realized I'd said the words out loud: "Does it bother you?"

He looked at me in the darkness. "Does what bother me?"

"That I'm gay?"

"No, of course not." He smiled, but it seemed as forced as his laughter a moment ago. "Have I ever given you a reason to think it did?"

"No, you haven't," I said. "I don't know; I guess I've just wondered. Ever since you agreed to move in."

"Would I have moved in if it did?"

I shifted uncomfortably. "Well, I mean, we're both in kind of dire straits these days. Beggars can't be choosers and all that. So I wasn't sure if it bothered you. Especially having your son living with me."

"Why should it?"

"Well, it…." I caught myself, gnawing the inside of my lip as I debated how to finish the answer.

"Hmm?"

Though it was barely visible in the darkness, I watched my thumb trace the edge of the label on my water bottle as I continued struggling to put my thought into words.

"Look," Michael went on, "if I had any issue with people being gay, Seth and I wouldn't have been friends this long. He wouldn't have put up with it."

"Oh, no, of course," I said. "I didn't mean to imply straight men are, by default, homophobic. You're obviously not. But I've, in the past, known some guys who were completely cool with it until sleeping arrangements came into play."

Michael laughed. "Well, it's not like we're sharing a room."

"No, that's true." *Unfortunately.* "I, fuck, I don't know. I guess it was a stupid question. I'm kind of used to straight guys being… uncomfortable with the idea."

"Nah, it's not a stupid question. If you're used to weird reactions, I can see being on guard for anyone to react that way."

Silence fell again. After I'd given our now-deceased conversation an awkward turn, I wasn't sure what to say to get us back on a more comfortable topic. Maybe it was better to let it be. Go inside, call it a night, and see if the awkwardness followed us into the next day.

I took a breath, fully intending to bow out, but he spoke before I could.

"Do you ever question it?"

I furrowed my brow. "Question what?"

"The fact that you're gay?"

"Not anymore."

"But you did?"

"Of course I did." I laughed. "Who wouldn't? I don't think anyone volunteers for the crap we put up with, so I had plenty of 'are you sure about this?' conversations with the mirror."

"But you always came to the same conclusion."

I nodded.

"Were you ever…." He paused, gazing out at the yard again instead of at me. "Did you ever date women?"

"No. A lot of guys do—shit, didn't Seth date the prom queen when you guys were in high school?"

"Yeah, he did. Lucky son of a bitch."

"I think I'd have preferred the prom king, but hey, more power to him."

"Yeah, really," Michael said quietly. "You know, I've always wondered if he was experimenting or if he knew and was trying to hide it from his parents."

"He was out to you by then, wasn't he?"

Michael nodded. "Me, and no one else that I'm aware of. But he kept dating girls, so I…." He went silent for a long moment. "God, he was so scared of his parents finding out. It was hard to tell whether he was trying something for his own curiosity or as a cover story."

"Maybe it was a little of both."

"Maybe." Michael tilted his head back and stared up at the stars. "So you never experimented with women?"

"Nope." I followed his gaze upward. "By the time I was even interested in dating, I knew I had zero interest in women."

"That must have been... I don't know, a relief, I guess."

"What do you mean?"

"Knowing for sure."

I rolled the comment around in my head. "I guess it was. I mean, I still questioned it just because I wasn't keen on the idea of coming out, but I never could convince myself I was attracted to women."

"What happened when you came out?" he asked. "Was your family supportive?"

To this day, it choked me up a little, thinking about how scared I was before and how relieved I was after I'd said those two unretractable words to my parents. *I'm gay*, my younger, slightly higher voice still echoed in the back of my mind. *I'm gay.*

My parents had been stunned. Totally taken aback. Never had a clue. It definitely blew their minds for a few terrifying minutes. But after those minutes, when the truth had sunk in, my parents told me they loved me and that had not and would not change.

"They were saints," I whispered.

"You're lucky," he said, his voice no louder than my own.

"Believe me, I know." I turned toward him. "I remind myself of that every single day."

Michael said nothing.

Chapter 11

WHEN I came home one evening from running errands, Seth's truck was in the driveway. I found him and Michael in the living room, talking shit over a video game with beer bottles—one in front of Michael, three in front of Seth—on the coffee table.

They looked up as I came in, and Seth gestured with his controller. "Hey, man. You want to play?"

I shook my head. "No, I think I'm going to go out and—" My eyes darted toward Michael, and warmth flooded my cheeks. I cleared my throat. "I've been putting off some admin work I need to finish at the club. I should go get it done before it keeps me awake for another night."

Michael glanced at me, eyebrows up, but quickly focused on the game again.

I turned to go, adding over my shoulder, "I'll see you guys later."

"You work too much," Seth called after me as I started toward the stairs. "Going to be an old man before your time."

"That's why I have mature friends like you," I called back. "Keeps me young and stupid."

"I live to serve!"

Chuckling, I headed upstairs and into my bedroom, where I changed into something a little more presentable than faded jeans and an old T-shirt. Still jeans, but with a button-up shirt and a silver chain that rested across my collarbones. My lucky chain, as Wes had always called it. Don't know about that—after all, I was wearing it when I met him.

I went downstairs and made a quick exit, but when I drove out of the quiet cul-de-sac, I didn't go anywhere near Lights Out. Yeah, the books needed attention, but I wasn't behind on them for once, and concentration wasn't happening tonight. I needed an evening to myself to clear my head.

So instead of driving to Lights Out, I went to the opposite end of Hacktown, to Jack's. This place might have been one of my biggest competitors, but I could be less covert about being on the prowl here than in front of members of my payroll, where I could certainly hook up as long as I was very, very discreet.

I parked on the street and walked the half block to the club. At the door, a bouncer took five dollars for the cover charge and gestured for me to go on in.

Though I hadn't been to this particular club all that often, it was familiar in the way all clubs eventually became familiar. The same neon signs for the same beer brands, from Budweiser to the local microbrews. The crack of pool balls occasionally punctuating the constant murmur of chatter and the thumping bass from the music playing beside the dance floor. Loners by the bar, couples in the corners, everyone else somewhere in between.

Empty booths and barstools outnumbered the occupied ones. Typical of a Wednesday. Friday or Saturday, there'd be far more options, but I couldn't get away from my own club on those nights, so the midweek crowd would have to do. And thin or not, the crowd offered plenty of choices: the cowboy wannabe in tight jeans and a tipped hat, the wide-eyed and terrified college kid probably setting foot in a gay bar for the first time, the fortysomething with five-hundred-dollar highlights. Even after I'd weeded out the too young, the too aggressive, and the too married—hey, I had standards too—there was no shortage of the willing and the good-looking.

I was in no hurry. I had what I wanted—an escape from home—and I'd find someone before the bartenders called last call. For the patient man, this place was a one-night stand waiting to happen.

I took a seat at the bar and continued scanning the crowd. Some of these guys were familiar. Hell, most gay men in Tucker Springs had probably come through the door of Lights Out at one time or another, so of course I'd recognize some faces. Maybe they'd recognize me, maybe they wouldn't. It had been known to happen. I almost always found out after the fact that they were more attracted to my wallet than me, but we both usually got a decent night out of the deal before I caught on that he was a gold digger and he realized I was severely lacking in gold.

I recognized the bartender, and apparently it was mutual, because his expression soured after a second's worth of eye contact. Oh yeah. I remembered him. He'd interviewed for a bartending position at Lights Out a few months ago. I'd seriously considered hiring the kid until he opened his mouth and let his attitude show.

"Rum and Coke," I said.

"Rum and Coke," he repeated. "That'll be four fifty."

Even as I pulled out my wallet and withdrew a five and a one, I watched him mix the drink. He probably thought I was smugly scrutinizing his technique and reminding myself why I hadn't hired him. In reality, I wanted to make sure he didn't throw in a spitball or some pocket lint for spite. With the way his interview had gone, I wouldn't have put it past him.

He finished making my drink and slid it across the bar on a square green napkin. I paid, tipping him properly, and with my glass in hand, turned to take in the scenery.

I didn't need liquor to work up the courage to approach someone. As much as Michael could render me tongue-tied, I could hold my own when it came to the games men played between flirting and fucking.

The first to catch my eye was a guy with curly blond hair, over by the dartboards, but a tan line on the third finger ruled him out. Guy bending over the closest pool table? Cute ass, but way too young. I might have approached the one leaning against the wall, with the blue Mohawk and an "I'm too cool to be here" smirk, if I hadn't recognized him. The Mohawk had been yellow and about an inch shorter when I'd barred him for life from Lights Out last year for threatening one of my bartenders with a broken bottle. Spending a night with him? Yeah, no.

I took another drink and kept looking around.

Ooh, *he* was cute. Jeans that were as tight—and probably as thin—as a condom. Meticulously messed-up bleach-blond hair. Lips that were made for making out, and don't even get me started on blowjobs. He was more Seth's type than mine, though: not *quite* femme, but close. He was the kind of guy who could pique my interest but would have Seth weak in the knees. I almost wished Seth was here with me; he made a great wingman, and it always cracked me up to watch him go from snark and shit-talk to speechless and stumbling when a cute twink caught his eye.

But Seth was at my place. With Michael.

Michael. Who was straight. And perpetually shirtless. And wouldn't get the fuck out of my mind no matter how much I looked at other men.

I shook my head. As I took another long drink, I reminded myself there was no point in pining after my roommate. That was why I was here, damn it—to find someone who *did* play for the same team.

My gaze locked on a guy watching a game of pool, and my glass almost fell into my lap. Jesus. He was very familiar, but I couldn't quite place his face. Probably someone I'd seen around, but who cared, because holy fuck. It wasn't often I was willing to consider slipping out the back of a club and sucking a stranger off in an alley before I even knew his name, but a guy that hot? Show me to the door.

So, drink in hand, I crossed the club and joined him by the pool tables. He glanced at me, and a devilish smile said I might have a shot here.

"You look familiar." I gave him a quick down-up. "Have we met?"

He laughed, revealing a row of gleaming, flawless teeth. "You use that line on every guy?"

Chuckling, I shook my head. "I guess it sounded like a pickup line, didn't it?"

"Wasn't it?"

"No, I was serious. I swear I've seen you somewhere before."

He looked me up and down, grinning. "Well, I don't remember seeing you anywhere before." Our eyes met, and he winked. "What a pity."

I smiled. "Definitely a pity." I extended my hand. "I'm Jason."

"Ray." He shook my hand. "So at the risk of using a cheesy pickup line of my own, you come here often?"

"This place? No. I'm… not much of a club guy."

"Neither am I." He glanced at our surroundings. "It's either clubs or the internet, though, and I haven't had much luck with that." He sighed, shrugging with one shoulder. "Which leaves either this place or Lights Out, and"—he grimaced—"yeah, I'll take this place."

Any other night, I'd have asked him to dish on Lights Out, and then dropped the bomb that I owned it just to see how fast he'd backpedal. Tonight? He could have insulted my mother and told me the Broncos sucked, and I wouldn't have budged.

Hot. Available. Gay. Matching opinions not required.

I shifted the subject away from the selection of gay clubs in Tucker Springs. The important thing was that he moved closer to me as the conversation went on. When I suggested finding a place to sit, he suggested one of the secluded booths at the other end of the room. In the booth, we played all the games: lingering eye contact, leaning in close enough to dare the other to move in for a kiss, a hand on the thigh.

And finally he threw the gauntlet.

"Do you want to get out of here?"

I grinned. "I was thinking the same thing."

Returning the grin, he pushed his empty glass away and slid out of the booth. I followed, and as I stood, I caught a glimpse of his face in profile, and *just* kept myself from letting go of an audible "Son of a *bitch*."

He was familiar? Yeah, he was. Jesus Christ, how the hell did I not figure it out from the moment I laid eyes on him? It was sure as fuck obvious now.

He looked like the goddamned roommate I'd come here to avoid.

Okay, so the resemblance was a passing one, but it was there. And truth be told, now that I'd made the connection, Ray lost a little of his luster because I couldn't stop comparing him to Michael. Not *quite* as fit. Not *quite* as tempting. Not *quite* such disarming brown eyes.

But he was hot, he was willing, and he was here.

"So," he said, "your place or mine?"

I licked my lips. "How about yours?"

"Let's go."

I GOT home around ten the next morning. My shoulder hurt, but after a night like that, what *didn't* hurt? That man was insatiable and definitely knew what he was doing.

By all rights, the itch should have been well scratched. I had the kind of libido that craved sex whenever I could get it if I was in a relationship, but could go significantly longer periods when I was single. In theory, I should have been set for a while after last night.

But I wasn't.

I'd have been home earlier—I tried not to overstay my welcome with one-night stands—but I'd driven around for a while after leaving Ray's place. Decided I needed coffee from a particular shop on the other side of Tucker Springs. Debated getting breakfast, but after driving clear down by the university to a particular restaurant, realized I wasn't interested in eating there after all.

When the clock on the dash said the coast was clear, that the man I'd been thinking about all night in Ray's bed had definitely left for work by now, I made my way home.

And there, in my driveway, was Michael's car. Fuck. Seriously?

Well, I couldn't drive around forever, and I did have a few things to get done before I went to work tonight, so I bit the bullet, parked, and went inside.

Michael looked up from rinsing out a tea mug as I dropped my keys on the counter, but he quickly turned back toward the sink.

"Morning," he said.

"Morning." I made myself a cup of coffee. "Shouldn't you be at work?"

"It's Thursday." His tone was flat, bordering on terse. "No appointments on Thursdays or Saturdays, remember?"

"Oh, right." And I knew that, didn't I? We'd lived together long enough, I should have picked up on the pattern, but I'd been so wound up the past few days, it hadn't crossed my mind he'd fucking *be here* this morning. So much for relieving some tension.

Leaning against the counter, I cradled my coffee in both hands as I tried like hell to keep the stiffness in my shoulder from showing. Having Michael treat me at home was fine and good, but I was pretty sure Ray had left a few marks. Michael might not give a fuck, but I would know, and that would be… awkward. So I moved slowly and carefully, willing myself to relax and not keep my left arm tucked against my side the way I did when it hurt.

Michael kept his attention focused on his task. Something was definitely amiss here. No one lounged the way Michael did when he was home, even when he was doing some work or on the verge of losing a game, but right now he stood ramrod straight. Jaw set, shoulders tight. His lips were pulled into a thin, taut line, and grooves between his eyebrows spoke of intense concentration.

Finally Michael turned off the faucet and cleared his throat. "Well, I'd better, um, get to the clinic. No appointments today, but I've got some paperwork to catch up on. You know how it goes."

Before I could comment, he was gone, leaving me staring over my coffee cup at the empty kitchen.

I slid my gaze toward the stairs. Floorboards above me creaked with movement, and my heart beat faster as something twisted below my ribs. Over and over in my mind, I watched him get up and walk out. In a hurry to get somewhere? Or in a hurry to get away from me?

I sipped my coffee, but I didn't taste it.

What the hell just happened?

Chapter 12

A T THREE thirty in the morning, it was lights-out at Lights Out. All that remained of the music was the inevitable ringing in my ears. The bartenders had cleaned up and clocked out, the servers and bouncers were long gone, and all that was left was to shut the doors and head home.

Another night, a few more drops in the coffers. It wasn't a bad shift, actually. Decent turnout, liquor flowing the way it needed to; by the looks of the closing slips from the tills, Lights Out might've even pulled a profit for a change.

After I swung by the bank and dropped the cash in the night deposit, I headed home, feeling pretty damned good for once. My shoulder didn't hurt much tonight, and I was looking forward to a solid night of sleep. I hadn't been in much pain in the three days since Michael had last treated me. Thank God for that—I was too exhausted to even put a hot pack on it.

When I got home, Michael's car was there, but there was another car parked on the street. Close enough to my driveway that it clearly belonged to a guest in my house, not my next-door neighbor's.

The house was dark, including Michael's bedroom window.

I cringed and swore under my breath. Add that to the growing list of things I hadn't seriously taken into consideration when he'd moved in.

Motherfucker. Bad enough that every time we talked while he didn't have a shirt on, my crush on him inched toward maddening. Hell, inched *past* maddening.

And now? I glared at the car beside the driveway. Now *this*.

But Michael lived here. He was straight, he was unattached, and if he wanted to bring a woman home, it was his prerogative, no matter how much it would test my sanity between now and daylight. Good thing a few of the earplugs I kept at the club had migrated home with me over time, so I could block out any enthusiastic noises that made it to my end of the hallway.

Once I was inside, I turned the dead bolt and reactivated the security system. The house was completely silent. No moaning, no bedsprings creaking. My ears were still ringing as they always were after work, but there wasn't a sound except my own footsteps on the way up the stairs.

Just in case, I pulled a pair of earplugs out of a drawer and kept them on the bedside table.

I closed my eyes, and not a single sound or muscle spasm disturbed me for the rest of the night.

I WOKE to the sounds of movement. Nothing earthshaking, but the slightest sign of life was enough to jar me awake.

They were discreet, I'd give them that, but in this house, sounds carried. What the bed frame didn't give away, the occasional muffled moan did. Though he wasn't particularly loud, Michael was definitely vocal. More so than his partner—I didn't hear her at all. Every once in a while, a faint vibration made it to my ears, a deliciously low timbre I felt more than heard. He had a sexy voice, and apparently it dropped even lower when he was turned on.

Torturing myself wasn't getting me anywhere, so I got up and went to take a shower. Though I could no longer hear them—him—I was acutely aware of what was going on down the hall. My mind showed me all kinds of images. Michael fucking her in every position imaginable. His eyes closing as her head bobbed up and down on his cock. Straight porn had never done a thing for me, but in this instance, all I could see was *Michael*. Aroused, sweaty, banging the hell out of someone. I'd seen his bare torso enough times, it didn't take much to add sweat and hands running down his back to the mental image.

Once I was in the shower, there was no point in pretending I wasn't turned on. Not when I knew Michael was having sex with someone right down the hall. Fuck, I couldn't remember the last time I'd gotten off that fast on my own.

By the time I was done, the house was silent again, so I moved as quietly as I could to keep from disturbing them. Always a challenge with hardwood floors and crap acoustics, but I did my best, opening the bathroom door slowly to keep the hinges from shrieking and stepping to avoid the boards that creaked the loudest.

Michael's bedroom door was closed. They probably hadn't left yet, not unless they'd finished, dressed, and gotten the hell out of Dodge in the time it took me to get in the shower, get off, and get out.

At just after ten—which was early as fuck for me—I was in the kitchen and halfway through my second cup of coffee when two sets of feet quietly came down.

They didn't come into the kitchen. At the bottom of the stairs, their footfalls went right and continued into the foyer. I released a relieved breath; there was nothing as awkward as bumping into a roommate's one-night stand—or first-time fuck, or girlfriend he hadn't mentioned until now, or whoever—the morning after.

In the foyer, Michael said something, and the reply made me choke on my coffee.

That wasn't Michael's voice, but it was damn sure a *male* voice.

I craned my neck, listening. The front door closed before either of them said anything more, but I'd heard enough.

Fuck. *Seriously*?

Jesus effing Christ on a skateboard. So that was why I didn't hear a woman's moans this morning.

Oh, you lucky motherfucker. I shivered as I re-played everything I'd imagined earlier, but with a man in place of a woman. Oh God. The thought of a woman's legs wrapped around his waist was noth-ing compared to a man's powerful legs hooked around Michael. A man's hands grabbing Michael's arms, Mi-chael's head going up and down over another man's cock....

Another shiver and I almost dropped my coffee. I set it down just to be safe and deliberately thought about the club's books to keep myself from thinking about Michael driving his cock into another man, or that man driving his cock into Michael, both of them moaning and shuddering and—

The books, Jason. Think about the books.

And then Michael came back in and the books in my mind went up in flames, leaving me with the fanta-sies of what he might have done earlier, and the reality of his gorgeous body right in front of me.

Our eyes met. From the heavy shadows beneath Michael's, I guessed he and his companion hadn't called it an early night last night.

Clearing his throat, he quickly turned away, but not before his cheeks turned pink. "I figured you'd still be asleep."

"It's after ten."

"Weren't you out until three or four?"

"Yeah, but that's still almost a full night's sleep."

He cocked his head. "Yeah, I suppose it is, isn't it?" He muffled a cough and turned away again, this time getting a bottle of water from the refrigerator.

I sipped my coffee. Ever the fucking masochist, I let my gaze slide down his shoulders and back. My heart skipped when I realized a shadow on his waist wasn't a shadow at all. God, they just had to fuck each other hard enough to leave marks, didn't they? Because my brain hadn't already had a field day *without* the use of visual aids like the bruise above his waistband or the hint of a mark on the base of his neck. At least he didn't have any bites, or I might have evaporated into a cloud of pure jealousy.

Weird, uncomfortable silence descended between us. He set the bottle down, the quiet tap echoing through the cavernous kitchen.

I wrapped my fingers around my coffee cup. Michael folded his arms and drummed his fingers rapidly on his upper arm. I looked at him only when I was sure he wasn't looking at me, but misjudged it and caught his eye when he glanced in my direction.

"So, um…." I managed to form two words but couldn't figure out how to follow them. *How was your night? How was he? Whatever he did, I would give my right arm for the opportunity to do better.* Maybe even, *Why the hell did you tell me you were straight?*

Michael played with the bottle cap on the counter. "I, uh…." He paused, keeping his gaze fixed on the floor. "I'm assuming you're all right with…." He gestured toward the stairs and raised his eyebrows as if he were begging me to put two and two together. Finally he added a whispered, "Guests?"

"Don't worry about it." I waved a hand, then reached for my coffee. "You live here, Michael. You're welcome to bring people around."

"Well, okay, I know, but…." He exhaled. "I guess I'm still getting used to the arrangement."

Tell me about it.

"Part of having a roommate, right?" I laughed, hoping it didn't sound as forced as it was.

He offered a thin, unenthusiastic smile, which quickly fell. "Listen, um…." He paused, clearing his throat. "I'm sure I don't have to ask, but you'll be…." His eyes darted toward the stairs, then back to me. "Discreet?"

"What else would I do?" I asked. "I'm not going to put your face on the bulletin board at the club or anything."

Michael chuckled halfheartedly. "Well, no, I didn't figure you would. But, I mean, my son doesn't know. And neither does Seth."

I'm wondering how long you've *known….*

"Secret's safe with me."

"Thank you."

Awkward silence descended again. God, so many things I wanted to ask him, most of which boiled down to *What do I have to do to get into your bed?* Fortunately I found some restraint, though when Michael headed upstairs to get a shower, I couldn't decide if I was relieved or kicking myself for not working up the nerve to say anything.

Usually I didn't care if a roommate got laid. In fact, having several over the years, I openly *encouraged* each and every one of them to fuck as often as humanly possible, because sexually satisfied roommates were easy to live with.

When that roommate was my every sexual fantasy personified? Then I wasn't quite so enthusiastic about him knocking the plaster off the walls.

"I'm sure I don't have to ask, but you'll be… discreet?"

I'd keep my mouth shut, but he'd definitely piqued my curiosity. Among other things.

My roommate was hot. My roommate rarely wore a shirt. And my roommate slept with men.

Want.

Chapter 13

I NEVER drank at work. Even if it were legal, which it wasn't, it was bad form and unprofessional. Tonight? Oh my God, it was tempting. Pour me some Jäger and let me go.

The kid was at his mother's. It was Saturday night. When I'd left for work, Michael had been on his way upstairs to take a shower. I had no idea where he would be or what he'd be doing. As far as I was concerned, the only question was *who* he was doing, and I envied the son of a bitch who wound up staying with him tonight.

At least I was here and not at home with my roommate. Since the night Michael had slept with another man in my house, I was halfway to bona fide, card-carrying, irreversibly crazy. I couldn't even look at him without hearing—*feeling*—the low, reverberating sounds that had come from his room that morning, and every creak of a floorboard made me think of squeaking furniture. The faint bruise above his hip had faded, but that didn't stop my mind from telling me every shadow that fell across his skin—always without his shirt, *always without his fucking shirt!*—was a mark left by some man who got closer to him than I ever would.

Frustration. Jealousy. Plain old horniness. Whatever the word, it was driving me out of my mind.

Thank God I'd be at work until nearly dawn, and hopefully Lights Out would keep me occupied and distracted so I didn't think about what was going on at my house.

Doubtful. The club wasn't setting itself up to be terribly stressful tonight. Quite the contrary: it looked a bit too quiet. On a Saturday night, people should've been standing in line outside and the bartenders' tip jars should've been overflowing before eight thirty.

I rested my hands on the bar and surveyed the scene. Rumor had it one of the other clubs in town was having some sort of event tonight, so that probably drew away a portion of my clientele. That, and we were getting into finals for both universities. Tucker U would be wrapping up next week, and East Centennial the week after that. Which meant students would be taking off in droves for summer vacation. Traveling, returning to wherever they called home, not coming through the doors of Lights Out.

In a university town, summer wasn't good for business.

Wasn't good for selection either, but I couldn't say I was terribly picky tonight. The one man I wanted was out of reach, so anyone else would never be better than second best anyway. Better than jacking off to futile Michael-shaped fantasies. Good thing I worked in a place where plenty of men came looking for someone to tangle up with all night before parting ways at dawn, because if I couldn't have Michael, then that was exactly what I needed this evening.

But for now, I had to run the club. I didn't leave until after closing, which meant there was no point in finding anyone now. If he was horny enough for a one-nighter, he wasn't going to hang around until three in the morning for me to come fuck him. On the other hand, whoever was left at the end of the night would be as desperate as I was. You scratch my back, I'll scratch yours; your place or mine?

In the meantime, business.

I made the rounds, checking on my bartenders and servers, making sure the DJ was set for the night, and keeping an eye on anyone who might be taking advantage of my liberal break policy. I asked the bouncers if they'd spotted any potential troublemakers. So far, so good.

On my way to the upper level, I took out the earplugs I always wore downstairs. It was loud up here, but it was the difference between watching an airshow and sticking my head inside the intake of a space shuttle. If Tucker Springs ever wound up with an epidemic of hearing loss among its young gay population, I would probably be partly responsible.

My eyes only took a moment to adapt from the flickering strobes downstairs to the dimmer, static lights up here. The older, more subdued crowd mingled and drank, shot pool and flirted, exchanged looks and phone numbers. Beer bottles. This or that on the rocks. Martinis. The bartenders undoubtedly pushing top-shelf. Quieter than downstairs, but not bad.

A face in the crowd caught my attention, and I stopped in my tracks.

Oh God.

Apparently there was something worse than knowing Michael was fucking other men in my house: when he came to *my club* to find those men.

Whatever gift he had for reading answers before they were spoken, he must have used it to tap into the part of my brain where I listed things that made my mouth water. Jeans that fit perfectly. Five-o'clock shadow. Hair arranged flawlessly but not locked into place with gel or some other shit that would preclude running my fingers through it. And of course the borderline fetish that Wes always thought was ridiculous—an old T-shirt under a blazer. Exactly the right amount of classy and casual mixed with some good old-fashioned don't give a fuck.

For the first time in my life, I was convinced someone had been put on this earth for the sole purpose of driving me *insane.*

And in case my blood pressure wasn't already all over the place, Michael saw me. And he was coming this way. And there was no pretending I hadn't seen him, because I was staring at him like an idiot.

"Hey," I said when we were barely an arm's length apart. "Didn't expect to see you here tonight."

He smiled and brought his drink toward his lips. "Yeah, I hope you don't mind me crashing your club."

"No, not at all." I forced a grin. "The more the merrier."

"Well, I've heard good things about this place."
His smile suddenly lacked its usual shameless confidence. "Thought I'd, you know, check it out."

"Hope it doesn't disappoint."

Over the rim of his glass, his eyes narrowed
slightly and locked on mine. "So far so good." As he
took a drink, though, that momentary confidence, that
flicker of boldness, faded, and he dropped his gaze.
Then he met my eyes. "Do you, um, have a few minutes? To go somewhere and talk?"

I smiled in spite of the knot that twisted beneath
my ribs. "I'm the boss. I can take a few minutes if I
want to."

His smile remained uncertain.

I nodded toward the stairs. "Come on."

Heart pounding, I led him out into the stairwell
and up to the employees-only rooftop terrace.

"There's a third level?" he asked.

"Well, not really," I said. "More of a glorified
break room for my employees. Sucks during the winter. Everyone has to take breaks in the storage room,
and the smokers? Well, they're pretty fucked." *And
you're rambling, Captain Smooth-N-Suave.*

Michael laughed. "Seems like a good way to motivate them to quit."

"That's what I've told them, but they just go outside and suffer."

He chuckled but didn't say anything.

We stopped beside the chest-high concrete railing, and when Michael looked up at the night sky, so
did I.

Tucker Springs didn't have the same amount of
light pollution as places like Denver, and when the

night sky was this clear, the stars were more visible than they had any right to be over a city. Not the way they would have been if we were out in the middle of uninhabited nowhere, but still impressive. Something to stare at besides each other. But stargazing meant not talking, which defeated the purpose of coming up here.

"So." I resisted the urge to squirm. "You wanted to talk about something?"

His fingers started drumming on the railing, marking a rapid, nervous rhythm on the weathered concrete. "About the other night."

"Okay...." I gulped. *Which other night?* I wanted to ask. *When you brought someone else home? Or when I came home with "I fucked another man" written all over me and you almost sprinted out of the room?* "Which part?"

Then, as abruptly as they'd started, his fingers stopped drumming. "I... don't even know."

Give me something here, Michael. A sign. A hint. Something.

Exhaling, he ran a hand through his hair but kept his attention fixed on the mountains instead of me.

"I thought you were straight." *Oh. Great. Perfect start to keeping the conversation from getting more awkward.*

But he whispered, "So did I." He took a deep breath, lowering his gaze to the parking lot beside the club. "I've been telling myself that for a long, long time, anyway."

If he'd had a finger on my pulse right then, he wouldn't have been able to count the beats. As he shifted and looked anywhere but right at me, I wondered if his heartbeat might have rivaled mine.

He closed his eyes and pushed out a breath. He might've even cursed softly, though I couldn't be sure. And finally he faced me and spoke. "To be blunt, I'm attracted to you." He broke eye contact again, adding a murmured, "*Very* attracted."

Oh dear God. Please don't let me be dreaming.

My mouth had gone dry, but somehow I whispered, "Likewise."

That didn't ease any of the tension in his posture. Or mine. Christ, where was this going?

Come on, Michael, give me something....

"So, if we both know we're attracted to each other...." I cleared my throat. "Then why don't—"

"It's not that simple."

"Isn't it?"

Michael moistened his lips. "I have to be careful of my kid. And there's my professional ethics. Yeah, we're roommates. We're.... We obviously...." He exhaled sharply. "But you're still my patient too."

"You could always treat me at home. I'll keep paying you just the same."

He kept his gaze down. "That wouldn't change much."

"You said yourself you've treated your ex-wife." I inclined my head. "And I don't imagine she was relegated to patient status after that."

Pursing his lips, he stared at the concrete between us. "No, she wasn't. But this is.... It's complicated. You're technically my patient. Plus we live together, so if things went south...."

"I'm not after a commitment ceremony and a joint mortgage, if that's what you're worried about," I said. "I've been there, done that."

He made eye contact at last. "Then what *do* you want?" It wasn't a demand, not when his eyes screamed, *Help me out, because I have* no idea *what's happening here.*

"I'm not even sure. I just want… you."

Turning his body so he faced me completely, he rested his forearm on the railing beside him. Though he leaned against the wall, his body remained tense. Twitchy. It was weird to see him like this. I wasn't used to Michael Whitman being flustered. Certainly not at a loss for words.

"It's not that I don't want to, Jason," he said finally. "Believe me, I do."

"Is that why you came here, then?" I asked. "To tell me why we can't do anything about this?" *When you're dressed for the prowl, when you're doing this here instead of at home, when you can't possibly fathom how much this is killing me….*

"I…."

I stepped a little closer, and we both tensed as the space between us shrank. "Michael?"

He slowly released a breath. "I needed to talk to you," he said, speaking quickly now, "and I'll be the first to tell you I suck at this sort of thing, so when I realized I needed to do it, I figured I should come down here and get it over with, but I hadn't really thought beyond pulling you aside to talk, so—" Abruptly, he cut himself off and shook his head. "Fuck, I don't know. Honestly?" He met my eyes again. "I don't know why I'm here."

"Are you sure about that?"

He swallowed. "No. I'm really not sure about anything right now."

"Except that you're here."

"Except that *you're* here."

Neither of us looked away this time. My heart thundered. Every muscle turned into a coiled spring waiting for one of us to trip my flight instinct. Or his.

But when would I have an opportunity like this again?

I'd never know where I found the nerve, but I reached for his hand on the railing. With only a few inches separating my palm from his skin, where his body heat started to mingle with mine, I paused. My fingers twitched indecisively in midair.

Michael's gaze darted toward that void between our hands. Then he met my eyes, and he'd never been so impossible to read. In the space of a heartbeat, his eyes told me to back off. The next, they dared me to keep going. The one after, begging me to pull back. Begging me *not* to pull back. And all the while, my unmoving hand hovered, waiting.

Finally, eyes still locked on his, I lowered my hand, but in the same instant, he pulled his out from under, and my palm landed on coarse, vaguely warm concrete.

Disappointment didn't even have a chance to register, because a split second later his concrete-cooled palm met the side of my neck and his lips met mine.

Neither of us moved. I couldn't, not until I'd found the equilibrium that went out from under me the instant our mouths made contact. Was this…. Had he really…. Did this really fucking *happen*?

God, yes, it did. And it wasn't over yet.

Michael's other arm slid around my waist. In-haling slowly through my nose, I wrapped my arms around him as our lips slowly, gently eased into motion.

Every first kiss since the dawn of time had ended much too soon, but not this one. Despite my desperate hunger for him, I couldn't see us doing this any way but slowly, sensually, one long breath at a time while the deepening kiss drew our bodies closer. Michael's hand rested on the small of my back, his other in my hair, fingertips unsteady against me as he nervously, confidently, shyly, boldly explored my mouth.

After an eternity, he drew back, breaking the kiss, but we didn't let go of each other, and damn it, I was wrong—it *had* ended too soon after all.

We held each other's gazes, both of us breathing hard and my heart pounding in my chest. Where we went from here wasn't as much of a foregone con-clusion as I'd have hoped; that kiss might have taken every reserve of confidence he had tonight, and a sin-gle step of retreat could stop it all. As the aftermath stretched out almost as long as the kiss that had pre-ceded it, I was sure with every passing second he was about to take that retreat. I was on the verge of beating him to it when his palm pressed into my back, and before I could make sense of anything, his lips were against mine again.

He wasn't so tentative now. Not so nervous. Quite the opposite, in fact, and I loved the way his mouth silently said, *I'm going to kiss you like this, and you're going to like it*, because I did like it. In that moment, I didn't think there was much I wouldn't have done if he'd demanded it. Not that I could think much at all, because his tongue teased mine, his fingers grasped my hair…. Oh God, I wanted him.

Panting and shaking, I pulled back and met his eyes. "We should go somewhere else. One of my…." I nodded toward the door. "My employees come up here sometimes."

Michael licked his lips. "Lead the way."

Without another word, I led him back to the stairwell and down to the hallway behind the upper club's bar. I keyed open my office, pausing to glance up and down the hall to make sure none of my employees were back here. We were alone, so I pushed open the door and we stepped inside.

The second the door was shut, Michael grabbed the front of my shirt and hauled me closer to him. I pinned him to the door, as much to catch my balance as to keep him right where I wanted him, and kissed him hungrily as he ground his erection against mine.

Stubble hissed across stubble, denim whispered across denim, and we both breathed sharply, rapidly, groaning into each other's mouths. God, this was even hotter than anything I'd imagined—I could barely believe this was real, that I was really tangling myself up in him and breathing him in.

I panted against his lips and held on to his shirt with one shaking hand, my other arm braced against the door behind him.

Michael ran the tip of his tongue across his lower lip. His pupils were blown, arousal written all over his wide eyes, but something else crept in, drawing his eyebrows together and loosening his grip on my shirt.

I gently cupped the side of his face. "What's wrong?"

"Look, I...." He took a deep breath. "I haven't done this. Not much, I mean."

"Which part?"

"Any of it." Color bloomed in his cheeks, and his grasp on my shirt loosened a little more. "The other night. When I brought someone home, that was...." He closed his eyes and swallowed hard. When he spoke again, the words came quickly and softly. "That was the first time I've ever been with a man."

My heart jumped. "Are you serious?"

Michael nodded, more color rushing into his face. With a dry, forced laugh, he said, "Better late than never, right?"

"Who said anything about late?" I combed my fingers through his hair and leaned in, seeking out his lips with my own. He hesitated at first, drawing back from me a little, but before I could pull away too, he curved his hand around the back of my neck and returned my kiss.

And abruptly, he pulled back and pressed himself against the door, swearing under his breath.

"You all right?" I asked.

"Nervous." He swept his tongue across his lips and avoided my eyes. "This...." He laughed softly. "It's ridiculous, but this... it scares me to death."

"Do you really want to do this?" *Please let his answer be yes, and please let him mean it.* My heart shifted into overdrive when his lips brushed mine and he whispered, "More than you can imagine."

His kiss backed him up, and I believed him.

I let my hand drift down his side, pausing at his belt, and when he shivered and his kiss intensified, I slid that hand between us.

Michael broke away with a moaned "Oh God."

My fingers found his zipper pull. "This okay?"

He nodded, wriggling against me as I opened his zipper. Closing his eyes, he exhaled hard and reached between us. I thought he might shove me away, but instead, he made a frantic, shaking attempt to unbuckle his belt. Since he was struggling, I took over. I finished what he'd started, and as my fingers slid into his jeans and boxers, Michael shivered again. I closed my hand around his thick cock, and a single thought nearly dropped my legs right out from under me.

Please, God, let him be a top.

I needed this man to fuck me. *Soon.* But first....

I went to my knees and took his cock into my mouth, goose bumps springing up along my spine as Michael released a low, throaty groan.

"Oh my God," he breathed. "Jesus, Jason...." He grasped my hair, tugging hard enough to make my scalp sting. I bobbed my head faster, both to give him more and to make him pull my hair even harder. I was dizzy with arousal, and every moan and curse encouraged me. When his breath caught, I was surprised I didn't come myself.

The floor vibrated beneath my knees, and in my mind's eye, I saw everyone downstairs on the dance floor, bodies moving together in time with the bass, with every thrumming beat that reverberated through me. Without realizing it, I'd fallen into the same rhythm as the music, and I moved with the pulsing beat the way the clubgoers did, and I imagined them getting closer to each other, touching and undulating, searching each other for the heat that crackled over their heads in the confines of my office. Hands sliding over clothes the way my supporting hand slid up the side of Michael's leg. Lips parted to release hot, ragged breaths like the ones Michael released as his fingers tightened in my hair.

The beat quickened. Intensified. Or maybe that was my blood in my ears. Whatever it was, it drove me on, and I stroked Michael faster and teased him with my lips and tongue, and his knee trembled beneath my other hand. One of us groaned, but I didn't know who because I was too fucking turned on to care.

Michael barely made a sound, just a deep, almost inaudible groan, but every soul in the building had to have felt his release. We must have sent a shockwave rippling through the club—blowing out speakers and bulbs, shattering bottles and glasses—in the same moment his semen flooded my mouth.

I sat back on my heels and swept my tongue across my lips as I gazed up at him. His eyes were closed, his head resting against the door, and he didn't look down when he spoke.

"Fucking Christ. I want to return the favor."

He didn't ask. He didn't suggest. Nervous and inexperienced or not, the undercurrent of his voice was bold and demanding, as if it was a foregone conclusion that we *would* leave this place, and he *would* return the favor, and we *would* have sex before this night was over. That kind of presumptuousness usually put me off, but from him, it was the single most arousing thing I'd ever heard.

So we got the fuck out of there.

Chapter 14

WE LEFT, but we didn't leave together. Michael went first, and as soon as he was gone, I slipped behind the first-floor bar and found Brenda in the back room.

"You mind closing tonight?" I asked.

She looked up from pulling a box of margarita salt off a shelf. "I thought your shoulder was doing better today."

"It was." I grimaced. "But... you know how it is."

She scowled. "You really need someone to look at that thing, Davis. You're not going to be able to move if it keeps up."

"Yeah, we'll see." With a little luck, I *wouldn't* be able to move tomorrow morning. Such was the plan, anyway, which meant it was time to get the fuck out of here. With Brenda at the helm of Lights Out, I made a quick escape and damn near busted my ass twice on the way down the back steps.

All the way from the club to my house, I was sure Michael would change his mind. God knew how much nerve it had taken him to come to Lights Out tonight, and in my experience, regret and hesitation usually came traipsing in shortly after the first orgasm subsided. Once the erection was gone, the mind was suddenly clear enough for doubts, and if those doubts showed up for Michael, then I would be rubbing one out in the shower tonight. Again.

But when I walked in the front door, Michael was waiting for me at the bottom of the stairs, and unless his eyes were lying, he hadn't changed his mind. Not at all.

I crossed the floor, mouth watering and cock already hardening, but right before I reached him, Michael stopped me with a hand on my chest. My heart didn't even have time to react before he gestured at the stairs.

"Up there." His voice was low and quiet. "Once we get started, I'm not stopping for anything."

Well, all right, then....

Without another word, we hurried upstairs.

As soon as we made it to the end of the hallway, within reach of his bedroom door, Michael spun around and grabbed the front of my shirt. We kissed with all the frantic hunger I'd expected out on the rooftop earlier: breathless, desperate, no idea what to do with our hands except grab on, hold on, *don't let go, please, God, don't let go.*

As I had in my office, I pinned him against the door, forcing his lips apart with my tongue. We gripped hair and clothes, pressing our hips together as we groaned into each other's kisses. I still couldn't

believe he was here, that we were doing this. Every
fantasy I'd ever had about him vanished from my
mind because not one of them could hold a candle to
the reality—simply being against him like this, kissing him while his hands ran all over my body, was
hotter than all the possibilities I'd imagined. Because
this was real.

Michael's hand left my arm, and my heart beat
faster when I heard his palm brushing the door behind
him as he searched for the doorknob.

I broke the kiss and touched my forehead to his.
"Are you sure about this?" I asked, panting against his
lips. "About—"

"Yes," he whispered. "God, Jason, please...."

He opened the door, and we nearly toppled to the
floor. I wouldn't have cared; he could fuck me wherever he wanted as long as he fucked me.

But we stayed on our feet, the hardwood floors
creaking beneath our stumbling footsteps. We inched
toward Michael's bed, and somewhere along the way,
my shirt landed beside us. His landed on top of it.
Shoes thumped, then hissed across the floor as we
kicked them out of the way. Belts jingled. Zippers
unzipped.

Michael flicked on the light beside the bed and
growled, "Want to... want to *see* you," before he
pulled me into another kiss.

I hooked my thumbs in the waistband of his jeans
and would have pushed them over his hips, but Michael hauled me down onto the bed on top of him.
Christ, he was hard. We both were, and I was halfway
out of my damned mind too. I pressed my hips against
his, groaning when his erection met mine through our

clothes and his hot skin met my chest and abs. We ground together, breathed together, dragging fingers through hair and breath out of lungs, and I could *not* get close enough to him.

I dipped my head to kiss his neck, and Michael moaned.

"I suppose now would be—" He sucked in a breath as I nipped his collarbone. "—a good time to ask if you're a top or bottom."

"Either." I kissed where his neck met his shoulder, flicked my tongue across that spot I'd been dying to taste, and started kissing my way toward his jaw. "You?"

"I'm—oh, God...." He dug his fingers into my arms. "I've only been on top. So far."

Whoever's up there listening right now? Thank you. Holy hell. Thank you so fucking much.

I raised my head and kissed him. "Does that mean I won't have to twist your arm to fuck me?"

"You can if you want, but I don't think you'll need to," he growled. "I want you so bad, Jason."

I bit back a whimper. "Do you?"

"God, yes." He kissed me again. Our mouths separated enough for him to add, "I want to fuck you," and I shuddered.

"Please do," I murmured against his lips before sinking into another deep, desperate kiss.

He slid his hand up my arm, and when I raised my head again, uncertainty creased his forehead. "Your shoulder," he breathed as his palm drifted over it. "I don't want...."

"I'm good. And right now, I couldn't care less." I'd regret it in the morning, but to hell with it. "Fuck, let's get out of these clothes before I go insane."

"Love that idea."

Another kiss was tempting, but then we'd never pull apart long enough to get undressed, so I pushed myself up. We threw off the rest of our clothes, letting them fall haphazardly on the floor.

As his jeans landed near mine, we stopped and stared at each other. Only an arm's length divided us as we stood beside his bed, looking each other up and down. I'd seen his bare torso a hundred times, I'd seen and tasted his cock, but the whole picture? Oh God. Nothing made a top more appealing than toned, powerful legs—they meant he could fuck like nobody's business, and with a cock that thick? Bring it the fuck *on*.

Our eyes met. The lift of his eyebrows hinted at the inexperience that made him hesitate before, but his dark eyes and ghost of a grin said nothing but "why aren't we back in bed yet?"

We fixed that situation in a hurry. He was on top this time, pinning me to the mattress and kissing me hard, exactly the way I loved it. *Fuck.* Inexperienced or not, this man was aggressive.

His lips left mine and descended on my neck, tracing a slow, warm path to the hollow of my throat. I shivered when his chin gently abraded my skin, and I gripped his shoulders as he worked his way back up the other side of my neck.

And back down again.

And farther down.

Farther, until my hands slipped off his shoulders and dropped to the bed beside me.

His eyes flicked up and met mine in the same instant he kissed above my hipbone, and my fingers curled around the sheets.

"I told you," he murmured, pausing to drop another kiss dangerously close to my rock-hard cock, "I wanted to return the favor."

With that, his mouth was on me, and my back lifted off the bed as I grasped the sheets even tighter. He was cautious at first, steadying my cock with his hand and running his tongue along the underside, around the head, back down. When he put his lips around the head, I moaned softly, and he took me deeper into his mouth. Not deep-throating—didn't imagine he was ready for that yet—but holy shit, this was perfect.

He sucked my cock with insatiable enthusiasm, and I closed my eyes, letting myself get lost in everything he did. With the way he kissed, it shouldn't have surprised me that he was this good with his mouth. He shouldn't have known exactly how to do this, how to circle the head of my cock with his tongue or squeeze just right with his lips and his hand, but he did, oh God, he did.

Combing my fingers through his wavy hair, I dug my teeth into my lip and struggled to stay still, to keep from forcing my cock into his mouth the way I desperately wanted to do. I wanted nothing more than to fuck his mouth, but he wasn't experienced—*Jesus, you'd never know it from the way he sucks cock*—so I held back. Tried to, anyway. My hips moved with no conscious effort on my part, lifting slightly off the bed and keeping perfect time with Michael.

All at once he stopped, and before I could protest, he pushed himself up on his arms and came up to kiss me.

"I can't wait," he said, panting between kisses. "I *need* to fuck you."

Even if my mouth hadn't been occupied, I wouldn't have been able to form any coherent words, so I deepened the kiss and moaned an affirmative. A low growl emerged from Michael's throat, and he pressed his hard cock against mine. I didn't care how inexperienced he was, he knew exactly how to drive me insane, and I wanted more, more, more.

He broke the kiss long enough for me to whisper, "Michael, please...."

Grinning, he came down and kissed me once more, briefly this time, before he lifted himself off me.

"We need a condom." I started to get up, but he stopped me with a hand on my arm.

"I'll get it." He released my arm and leaned toward his bedside table. When he returned with a condom and a barely used bottle of lube, some of his earlier uncertainty had crept back into his expression.

I sat up. "Hands and knees?"

He gulped. "Can your shoulder handle that?"

I cupped his face and kissed him lightly. "If it can't, we can always move. But I like it like that."

A smile flickered across his lips and, a second later, fully came to life. "Tell me if you want to change positions."

"I will, don't worry." I kissed him again and then sat back while he put on the condom and lube. Once everything was in place, I moved onto my hands and knees.

He knelt behind me, resting a hand on my hip. For a moment I thought he'd hesitate, but then the mattress shifted slightly beneath us, and a second later, he pressed against my ass.

Closing my eyes, I exhaled, willing myself to relax because I needed him as soon as—

Ooh....

He pushed in slowly, carefully.

Oh God....

I'd been fucked plenty of times in my life, but I couldn't remember the last time a man had taken my breath away with that first long, penetrating stroke. My elbows shook beneath me. My spine threatened to collapse into tiny electrified bits. My eyes watered as Michael worked himself deeper inside me, and I whimpered when he slid across my prostate.

"This okay?" he asked.

"God, yes." I rocked back against him, and he moved faster. He ran his hands up and down my sides as his hips picked up speed. I was right about his legs. Sweet Jesus, the man could thrust. Hard and deep, exactly how sex was meant to be, and still I moaned, "Faster... fuck... oh, fuck, faster...."

He gripped my hips and fucked me faster. A vague twinge in my shoulder threatened to ruin everything, but I shifted my weight onto my other arm and used my now-free hand to reach down and grip my cock. I held my breath and fought to keep from falling apart, but I stroked myself anyway because the need to come was nearly unbearable. I teetered on the fine line between holding back and giving in. The man who'd walked shirtless up and down my hallways, driving me insane with pure, raw lust, was inside me, holding on to me, fucking me, whispering and cursing, and I wasn't about to bring this to an end a second sooner than I had to.

"Oh my God," he moaned. "Oh God, I'm gonna come...." His fingers dug in, but not enough to stop me from rocking harder against him, and I pumped

my cock faster and swore and trembled and finally released a helpless groan as I lost it, and seconds later
Michael forced himself as deep inside me as he could,
shuddered, and came.

And everything stopped. My heart pounded, my
arms shook, but otherwise, we were still. The room
was silent except for both of us trying to catch our
breath and, after a moment, the whisper of Michael's
hands sliding up and down my back, drawing lazy,
gentle lines along either side of my spine.

"I thought you said—" I paused, licking my lips.
"I thought you said you didn't have much experience."

"I didn't say I was inexperienced with sex." He
leaned over me, his sweat-dampened chest warming
my back. When he kissed my shoulder, I turned my
head, and he found my lips with his. "I said I didn't
have a lot of experience with *men*."

"You say that," I murmured. "Your cocksucking
skills say differently."

He laughed and kissed my shoulder again.

After he'd pulled out, we both stood on shaking
legs and, once we'd cleaned up, sank back into bed
together.

He closed his eyes, brushing a few droplets of
sweat off his temple.

"So the other night," I said. "That really was your
first time with a man? Ever?"

Michael nodded slowly, and his cheeks darkened.

"Mind if I ask why?"

"Why it took me so long to sleep with a man?"
He turned toward me. "Or what made me do it now?"

"Both, I guess."

Michael chewed his lip. After a long moment, he said, "This sounds incredibly stupid, but... hear me out."

I nodded.

"I've known for a long, long time I was attracted to men, but I didn't want to be, especially after spending so much time and energy convincing people I wasn't. It's only the last couple of years I've started to accept it. And it wasn't....." He took a deep breath. "It wasn't until recently that I've worked up the nerve to sleep with one."

"So why now?"

His voice was soft, bordering on inaudible. "I wanted to know for sure if I liked being with a man. I didn't want to...." He paused, his eyes losing focus for a second. "I needed to try it with someone else first."

"First?" I swallowed. "Before... what?"

He swallowed as he lifted his gaze to meet mine. "Before this."

My heart jumped.

Michael moistened his lips. He rolled onto his back and stared at the ceiling. "I was attracted to you from the start, and I'd been telling myself over and over there were all these reasons we couldn't do this. But then after you came home that morning and I had a feeling you'd been...." He shivered. "I don't know, my imagination got the best of me, and I couldn't get you out of my mind. Then it occurred to me, I'd never actually been with a man. Even though I've known for a long, long time that I'm interested in men, how did I know if I was really comfortable sleeping with one?" His Adam's apple jumped. "I didn't want to sleep with you, find out I really *wasn't* into it, and then have things be awkward between us. Since we have to, you know, live together."

"So you gave it a try with someone else first?"

Without looking at me, he nodded.

"That's…." I shifted onto my side and propped myself up on my arm. "I think I can understand that."

"Really?" He finally turned toward me. "It sounded kind of ridiculous to me. In hindsight anyway."

"No, it makes perfect sense. If you weren't sure, hell, why not?" I put a hand on his chest, idly running my fingertips through the thin, dark hair. "I'm guessing you enjoyed it? With him?"

He laughed softly. "Yeah. But I didn't tell him I was thinking about you the entire time."

My fingers stopped. "You were?"

"You were the whole reason I went looking for him in the first place." His hand rested over the top of mine. "Of course I was thinking about you."

I swallowed hard. "I hope the real thing wasn't a disappointment, then."

Michael smiled. Reaching for my face, he lifted his head off the pillow and moved in to kiss me. Right before our lips met, he whispered, "There was nothing disappointing about it."

Chapter 15

I WOKE up to an arm draped over me and soft lips between my shoulder blades. Usually Michael was awake and out of bed long before me, but when the morning light drew me into consciousness, here he was.

"I didn't fuck up your shoulder last night, did I?" he murmured against my neck.

"Not at all." I smiled. "It feels fine."

"Sure about that?" He slid his hand over my shoulder, and I instinctively ducked away.

"It's fine. A little sore, but I'll be all right." I started to roll over, and he lifted his arm until I'd settled onto my back. Running my fingers through his disheveled hair, I said, "For the record, I don't think my shoulder's any worse for the wear. Rest of the body is a little sore, though."

He grinned. "Mine too."

"Mission accomplished?"

Michael leaned down to kiss me. "Mm-hmm."

Chuckling softly, I lifted my head to look at the clock. "It's almost nine. Since when do you sleep this late?"

"Are you trying to throw me out of bed?"

"Not at all." I ran my hand down his arm. "But you're usually up and gone by this time."

He shrugged. "And I probably should be. I have so much I need to do today." His hand drifted down my chest and under the covers. "But right now, I think most of that can go to hell."

"Is that right?"

"It is." He teased my hardening cock with his fingertips. "I finally got you into bed. I'm in absolutely no hurry to get you out of it."

"I do love the way you think." I pulled him down to kiss me.

It was a good half hour before we finally dragged ourselves out of bed and shuffled downstairs for some coffee.

I ignored the persistent ache in my muscles. No way was I complaining about this kind of discomfort. Spending an entire night in agony was one thing. Spending it letting Michael fuck me seven ways from Sunday and being a little sore the next day? That was well worth it. It was even worth the pain in my shoulder, especially since the cause was also the cure. Damn good thing Michael kept some of his tools of the trade at home.

But if there was one thing I'd learned the hard way over the last few years, it was that something this good was almost always—no, *always*—too good to be true. I should have known it wouldn't last. And maybe I did, but I thought I'd at least make it through a cup of coffee first.

Nope. Not a chance. That had to be some kind of record.

We stood on opposite sides of the kitchen, shirtless and clinging to our coffee cups. Michael didn't look at me. Neither of us said a word.

After a couple of uncomfortable minutes, he glanced at me but quickly shifted his gaze away.

Damn it. We were two swallows into a pot of coffee and he already regretted this, didn't he? I sighed. My stomach wound itself into knots as my own regret elbowed its way in, along with a hefty side of awkwardness.

"Might as well just come out with it," I said over my coffee cup. "Clear the air now before things get weird."

His eyes darted toward me.

Okay, so much for *before* things got weird.

Exhaling hard, Michael rested his hip against the counter and rubbed his eyes with his thumb and forefinger. "All right. Well, when it was only you and me in the house, it was no big deal, but…." He gestured at the stairs. "It isn't just us. And I guess I don't know if I can do this."

"Why not?" I asked. "Do you…. You don't think I'd throw this in his face, do you?"

"No, no, it's not that. But…." He blew out a breath. "Fuck, I don't even know why it's bothering me so much. I thought I wanted this. And I do. I really do. But we live together. With my kid. And you're my patient. And I'm…." He closed his eyes as he ran a hand through his hair. "I don't know. Last night was great, but now that I can think clearly, I... I just don't feel right about it."

I chewed the inside of my cheek. I wanted to argue that we could work around every one of those things, but... could we?

I took a breath and said quietly, "So we'll go back to being roommates, then?"

"I don't see what choice we have."

I bit back the obvious option.

"Dating someone is one thing," he said. "Living together, with my kid in the house...."

"We don't have to do anything while he's here."

"He's not stupid," Michael said flatly. "We don't have to be all over each other for him to figure out something's going on."

"I'm not suggesting he's stupid, but that doesn't mean—"

"Jason, we *really* shouldn't do this." Sighing, he sagged against the counter. "I'm sorry. It's not that I don't want to take it any further, but...." He rubbed his eyes. "I have to think about my kid. And with us living together, things could get really complicated."

My heart sank into my stomach. "Living together will also complicate things if we decide to back off."

"So are we obligated to keep it going?" he asked. "Because we live together?"

"Not at all. All I'm saying is it'll be complicated either way." I hooked my thumbs in the pockets of my jeans to keep myself from folding my arms. "We can't exactly go back and erase everything that happened last night."

"No, I suppose we can't." He rubbed his forehead. "The thing is, my kid doesn't even know I'm
gay. I barely admitted it to myself until recently. How
the hell do I explain any of this to a seven-year-old?"

"Are you ashamed of it?"

"What?" He shook his head. "No, of course not.
I...." Lowering his gaze, he released a breath. "I mean,
I'm not sure. I really don't know how I feel about it.
About... any of it."

I didn't respond. I didn't know how.

Keeping his voice so low I could barely hear him,
Michael went on. "It goes beyond telling him I'm gay.
Even dating is fucking complicated these days. I'm
always worrying less about the relationship itself and
more about how it'll affect my kid, which pretty much
sabotages things, and...." He trailed off.

"And I probably empathize with Dylan more than
you think," I said. "My parents are divorced and both
remarried while I was a kid."

He shifted a little, eyebrows up. "And was it difficult for you?"

I shrugged. "Of course it was. But it wasn't the
end of the world."

"And how would it have been if one of your parents were gay?"

"I don't know. Maybe it would have made a difference, maybe it wouldn't have. But I did want my
parents to be happy."

Michael sighed. "Which Dylan definitely wants.
I think it's been harder on him than me when I've
split with people." He paused. "The last time I broke
up with someone, it was completely amicable, and

honestly, I think that made it even harder on Dylan than if he'd heard us fighting."

I cocked my head. "How so?"

"It confused the hell out of him. I mean, we'd kept all of our arguments out of his sight. And as I said, it was amicable. We told Dylan we weren't getting along and needed to go our separate ways, but to a five-year-old, that didn't make any sense. He'd never seen us not getting along, so as far as he could see, things were fine."

Michael sighed. "His mother and I have always been on friendly terms too, and we've been apart as long as he can remember. So he doesn't know how to deal with relationships. His mom and dad have never been together. His dad's only girlfriends have left with, as far as Dylan's concerned, no warning. That's why he's never been able to bond with his stepfather. He's scared to death that any day now he's going to come home and Lee will be gone."

Closing his eyes, he scrubbed a hand over his face and swore under his breath. "The fact that you and I are living together only makes it that much more complicated. For Dylan and for me."

"And me."

"And you," he said with a subtle nod. "Look, I know I'm probably making more out of this than I should, but... I'm sorry." He avoided my eyes, and drawing back against the counter, he widened the gap between us by a short but decisive distance. "I'm not ready for this. Not right now."

I swallowed but didn't say anything. What could I say? It didn't matter how much it disappointed and frustrated me. I should have known this wouldn't be as simple as falling into bed and everything being perfect from there on out.

"I should…." He cleared his throat. "I should get to the clinic. Finish up some paperwork. And I promised Dylan I'd take him out to eat tonight, so I'll be home a little later than normal."

I just nodded.

He went upstairs. Not ten minutes later, he was out the front door and the house was empty.

Alone, I released my breath and slumped against the counter. I could not catch a fucking break. Especially since I couldn't seem to stop putting myself into situations where—

No. Not going to spend the day wallowing in self-pity. Wading in it, maybe, but not wallowing.

I went upstairs for a shower. Body still aching from the kind of sex we'd just agreed not to have anymore, I closed my eyes and let the hot water run over me while I replayed our conversation.

How could I argue with a man who wanted to protect his kid? I remembered what it was like when my parents started dating other people, and I lost enough sleep these days without being the reason a little boy was upset.

But now what the hell did I do? This didn't change how I felt about Michael. It didn't change the fact that I was more attracted to him than I could ever remember being to any man, especially now that we'd had the kind of sex I'd craved forever.

But our professional and housing arrangements complicated the sex. And the sex complicated our relationship as roommates and as doctor and patient. I needed the acupuncture. We both needed the house.

Two needs trumped one want, so the only thing we could cut was the sex.

No matter how good last night had been or how much I wanted to do it all over again.

Absently rubbing my shoulder beneath the hot water to keep pain from creeping in, I whispered a string of profanity.

Just once in my life, couldn't *something* be simple?

And for the first time, I regretted having Michael move in.

Chapter 16

By all appearances, Michael and I adapted back to platonic roommates without missing a beat. We passed in the halls. Played video games together—nonviolent when Dylan was with us, violent as all hell the rest of the time, especially when Seth was there. Took turns with various tasks in the house and the yard. Talked in the kitchen, the living room, out on the deck as if nothing had ever happened upstairs.

But all the while, the walls closed in. Inch by inch, day by day, the house shrank. The halls narrowed. The distance between his bedroom door and mine shortened, and in spite of the decreasing space, the echo of every creak, every step, every movement was amplified. No matter where Michael was in the house, I was hyperaware of him.

I needed to relieve this tension, but I was afraid of Michael overhearing me. Two single men living together, there was bound to be some jerking off once in a while, but he knew I was attracted to him now, so he'd put two and two together and figure out he was on my mind. Either way, I couldn't even relax myself with a little desperately needed masturbation.

And then there was the issue of my shoulder. Naturally, I'd reached the point where I could somewhat comfortably afford my appointments. I could pay Michael without cutting into my food budget or visiting El's pawnshop. Effective treatment was available and accessible for the first time since I'd fucked up my shoulder, but nothing aggravated the muscles like stress, and even the acupuncture wasn't helping now. Or, rather, the *acupuncture* helped, but the acupuncturist's presence countered everything his treatments offered. Alone in a dark room? With my shirt off and Michael's hands on me? What wasn't there to wind me up, stress me out, and turn my shoulder into a bright red beacon of *holy fuck that hurts*?

So I called and canceled my next two appointments.

"Do you want to reschedule?" Nathan asked. "I can schedule as far out as the end of July if that helps."

"Not right now," I said. "But thanks." Maybe I'd check into one of the other acupuncturists in town. Eventually. After I figured out how to explain that to my roommate.

Three days after my second canceled appointment would have happened, Michael came into the kitchen while I poured my morning coffee at quarter to noon.

He folded his arms loosely across his bare chest and stood in the doorway. "Hey."

"Hey." I made myself focus on pouring my coffee. On doing something other than facing him. Especially while he was standing there being all half naked and goddamned attractive.

"How's your shoulder?"

I resisted the urge to roll it to prove I could move just fine. Especially since I *couldn't* move just fine. Without turning around, I said, "It's fine."

"You know I can see it from here, right?" he said. "The muscle's tense. You're favoring it badly. You're holding your arm like—"

"What do you *want* me to say?" I snapped, turning to face him.

He jumped, his eyebrows climbing his forehead. "Jason, I want to help you. You're obviously in—"

"Yes, I'm in pain." I leaned against the counter and gripped its edge. "It fucking hurts, all right?"

Michael exhaled. "Then why not let me help you with it? If it's a money issue, we—"

"It's not the money," I said. "I can't… I can't do it."

He cocked his head. "But *you're in pain*."

"Thank you, I hadn't noticed," I muttered.

His eyes narrowed slightly. "If there's something I can do, then say so, and I will."

I stared at the floor, silently debating letting him treat me or telling him why I couldn't let him touch me.

"Jason?"

I swallowed. "Honestly?" I took a breath and mustered every bit of willpower I had to look him in the eye. "Having you treat me is only making it worse."

His eyes widened. "I thought you said it was helping."

"It is. Well, was. The acupuncture helps, but…."
You drive me insane. When you touch me, I want to touch you. Just standing here talking to you this way is making the muscle spasms worse because I'm going out of my ever-loving mind.

He pushed himself off the doorframe and took a step toward me but stopped when I drew back. He slid his hands into his pockets. "Is this about what happened between us?"

"Of course it is," I whispered. "When you work on me, it helps, but then I get so goddamned wound up from having your hands on me…." I made a sharp, frustrated gesture and avoided his eyes. "It pretty much cancels out whatever the needles have done."

"I didn't realize this was bothering you that much."

"It is." I lifted my gaze and met his eyes for a fleeting second. "So, yes, my shoulder hurts. But going to the clinic or having you treat me here, it isn't helping. I mean, it's bad enough wanting you the way I do when you don't want—"

"I never said I didn't want you." Michael came closer, shrinking the space between us to less than an arm's length, and when I drew back, my shoulder blades met the wall. "For what it's worth, it's been killing me too." His voice was unsteady. "If you think this has been easy for me, think again."

I closed my eyes and released a frustrated breath.

"Jason, I want you so bad, but this is…."

"If avoiding it is driving us both this crazy, maybe it's not as wrong as you think it is."

"I'm not saying it's wrong. I've never said it was wrong."

"So if we didn't live together with your son and you had never been my acupuncturist...." I moistened my lips. "Would we?"

"In a heartbeat," he breathed as he reached for me. The gentle pressure of his hand on my waist pushed the air out of my lungs. "If those factors weren't in place, God only knows what we'd have done by now."

Goose bumps rose along my arm as I touched his. "But those factors are in place."

"Yes." He wrapped his arms around me. "They are."

I traced the edge of his jaw with the backs of my fingers. "Which means we can't."

Michael nodded.

I couldn't make myself draw my hand back. I could barely make myself form the words, "Then why are we doing *this*?"

"I don't know." His voice shook, and he touched his forehead to mine. "All I know is, I want you right now."

"What do we do about tomorrow?"

He swallowed, pulling back and looking me in the eye. "We'll... figure that out when we get there. Right now I can't think beyond, well, right now."

I knew it was a bad idea. I knew I'd regret it. I knew I'd be kicking myself as soon as it was over because this would only make it that much harder to get him out of my mind.

But I kissed him anyway.

We stumbled. Holding on to each other, breathing in rapid unison, we nearly tripped over each other's feet before I found the counter and leaned against it for support. Now that we had gravity and support taken care of, the kiss deepened and intensified, his thickening erection pressing against mine and weakening my knees.

His hands slid under my shirt and across my skin. The heat of his touch made me shiver, and I arched my back, which pushed my body closer to his. I reached up to run my fingers through his hair, and that simple movement ignited a twinge in my shoulder.

A twinge that drew my attention away from his kiss and to the pain that had sparked this whole conversation. The pain that needed the acupuncture I couldn't get because I couldn't deal with Michael touching me because he wouldn't touch me any other way. Except now. This time. This *one* time.

And after this, what?

Nothing had changed. The reasons he balked at this still existed, which meant once the dust settled and the orgasms had peaked and fallen, we'd be back to where we were at the beginning of our conversation.

And if we did take this upstairs, I wasn't sure I could handle his disappointment when my shoulder kept us from going quite as wild as we had the first time. He knew damn well I had chronic pain, but accepting that in theory and accommodating it in the bedroom were two very different animals.

"Really?" I heard Wes in the back of my mind as Michael's fingers pressed into the back of my neck. *"If you're not in the mood again, just fucking say so."*

"It's not that." I parted my lips for Michael's insistent tongue. *"You know it isn't."*

Michael pressed me against the counter, and Wes's phantom voice growled in my ear, *"If it's that bad, take a fucking pain pill. I'm going to take a shower."*

"Wes, Wait...."

As the slamming door echoed in my mind, I broke the kiss and pulled away from Michael. "Wait. Stop." I gently freed myself from his embrace and sidestepped out from between him and the counter. "I can't do this."

He stared at me, hands still hovering in midair between us, and I couldn't tell if he didn't believe me or hadn't heard me right.

"I'm sorry. I... I can't." I took a step back, putting up my hands to keep him from closing the distance I'd created. "I know you want to protect Dylan. I know you're concerned about the whole doctor-patient thing. And I get it. We can't have a relationship. One that's a hundred percent sexual or... or isn't. We can't. I get it." Hands still up, I took another step away. "But I can't have you for one night and then pretend I don't want you every night after that."

Before he could give me a reason to stay, I turned and walked out of the kitchen.

THINGS ONLY got worse. Two steps forward, ten steps back. We'd given in once and crossed a line, and the second we'd separated, we were farther apart. The house's walls closed in tighter and tighter the more Michael and I tried to avoid each other.

Every minute in that house was driving me insane, so whenever I had the chance, I got the hell out of there. I spent hours at the club. Hung out with Seth whenever possible. Anything and everything that didn't put Michael and me in each other's crosshairs.

Tonight, when I left, I didn't have a conscious destination in mind, but when I stopped the car, I wasn't

surprised by where I was. After all, in spite of my hurry to vacate the house, I'd taken the time to grab a
shower, make myself presentable, and double-check
my reflection in the rearview before I'd pulled out of
the driveway. I had on a bit of cologne, and my lucky
silver chain rested across my collarbones. Where *else*
could I have had in mind?

I locked my car and walked into Jack's.

The guys were hot, as they always were, and more
than a few had stripped down enough to show off the
beginnings of their presummer tans. Tight leather,
tight denim, tight shirts. Grins and winks, suggestive
looks, pickup lines—*his next drink is on me.*

Now that I was here, perusing the faces and butts
to see if anyone looked attractively distracting or dis-
tractingly attractive, it occurred to me that this might
not be the best way to get Michael off my mind. It
was one thing to use sex to ignore my financial issues
or whatever other drama had parked itself in my reality. It was an entirely different one to use sex I sort
of wanted as a diversion from sex I really wanted. It
was like killing a craving for expensive wine with that
boxed crap they sell at the grocery store. It scratches
the itch but mostly makes you think of what you're
not getting.

It worked once, though. Well, kind of. I couldn't
say I'd gotten Michael out of my mind that night, but
at least I'd gotten laid. An orgasm was nothing if not a
momentary distraction. A *very* momentary distraction.
And at this point, I'd take what I could get.

But I couldn't even tell the attractive men from
the unattractive ones tonight. They all blended together. From the super-highlighted hair to the flashy shirts

to the skintight pants, they blurred into one colorless, featureless scene devoid of what I was really looking for. There were no cowboy wannabes, no twinks, no my type or Seth's type. Just a gray sea of drinking, undulating, dart-throwing *not Michael*.

Sighing, I turned back toward the bar. Who the hell was I kidding? This wasn't a night when any warm body would take the edge off. It was Michael or no one.

No one it is.

I pushed away my barely touched drink, dropped a five next to it for the bartender, and left, but I didn't go straight home. With the window down and the radio blasting, I drove around town. To the Light District. Up north by Tucker U. Down to the south end by East Centennial State University—East Cent, as it was called. I went by a few clubs that looked promising, if only for an evening of smooth jazz and cold beer.

No, too restless. Too wound up. Jazz could usually relax me—and there was plenty of it in this town—but tonight I was sure it would just remind me of how much I *couldn't* relax.

I had to go home eventually. At around ten thirty, I gave up looking for a reason not to.

Michael's car was in the driveway. His bedroom light was on, which meant he was awake but presumably alone. Hopefully with headphones, and his door shut, and completely oblivious to my return. Unless of course he'd changed his mind. In which case, I hoped he was well aware that I'd come home.

As I quietly climbed the stairs, I didn't hear a sound besides my own footsteps. If not for the strips of light above and below his bedroom door, I wouldn't have thought anyone was here at all.

I closed my own door behind me. Lying back on my bed, I gave in to the fantasies that had been bouncing around in my mind all night. Hell, all week. Ever since I'd met him, if I was honest with myself, and doubly so since I'd touched him.

Closing my eyes, I suppressed a groan as my cock hardened in my jeans. I reached for my zipper, but that simple motion brought a nearly inaudible creak out of the bed frame. I froze, sure that the creak echoed loud and clear into Michael's room, painting him a mental picture of me lying here, hard-on and all. And if I moved, if I did anything at all, he'd see it, he'd know it, and he'd know why.

And on the eighth day, God created the shower so men like me could jerk off without detection.

I swung my legs over the side of the bed and got up.

In the bathroom, I turned on the water, out of habit setting the temperature as high as I could bear it. It stung my skin, and I instinctively turned so the falling water pounded my tender muscles.

My shoulder ached, but it paled in comparison to the other ache that needed to be relieved before I could even think of doing anything else, so I ignored the pain, braced myself against the wall with my left hand, and stroked my cock with my right.

I'd had just enough of Michael to know what he sounded like, looked like, tasted like when he was as turned on as I was now. I'd memorized every moan, every growl, the way his expression bordered on one of pain when he was close to letting go. My hand mirrored his strokes, squeezing and releasing wherever he would have if he'd been in this shower with me, kissing me with a mixture of boldness and uncertainty. The helpless moans and throaty growls when he fucked me. Hands and mouth that couldn't have been as inexperienced as they were.

God, Michael, I want you so, so bad....

My eyes rolled back, my knees buckled, and semen mixed with hot water in my hand. I released my breath and focused on holding myself upright. *Don't collapse. Don't collapse. No bruised kneecaps on top of everything else. Stay up.*

Eventually my legs stopped shaking. My vision cleared. I caught my breath and regained my balance. Hot water still rushed over my skin. My shoulder still ached.

And Michael was still in the other room. And I was still in here. I had the aftershocks of an orgasm tingling at the base of my spine, but it wasn't enough.

It wasn't nearly enough.

"JASON, WE need to talk."

I set my coffee cup on the kitchen counter, slowly released my breath, and turned around.

Michael leaned against the doorway, one thumb hooked in the pocket of his jeans.

It didn't take a genius to figure out what we needed to discuss. After days on end of palpable tension, someone had to give in sooner or later and break the silence.

Setting my shoulders back, I met his eyes. "Okay. Let's talk."

His Adam's apple jumped. "This arrangement, me living here, was supposed to take some pressure off both of us." He fidgeted. "But it seems like it's having the opposite effect."

"Yeah, I guess it's only made things worse."

Michael nodded.

"So what should we do?" I asked. "You live here, and we've... well, the point is, what's done is done."

"Yeah." He ran a hand through his hair and sighed. "I think the best thing right now is to let that go and move on. It happened, but...."

I winced. "But it was a mistake."

Avoiding my eyes, he nodded again. "Maybe this arrangement isn't such a good idea. If we can't live together without going crazy, then... maybe we shouldn't."

I lowered my gaze. Every part of me wanted to shoot that suggestion down and insist we could make this work, but....

"Maybe we shouldn't."

Michael shifted his weight. "Do you want me to stay?"

I looked at him. "I *need* you to stay."

He swallowed. "But is my contribution to the mortgage really worth"—he gestured at both of us—"this?"

Who said anything about the mortgage?

"Look, I...." Deflating a little, I leaned against the counter. "There's no easy answer to this. No, I don't want you to go, but I also don't want either of us to be miserable."

"Neither do I." He moistened his lips. "So what do we do?"

"We don't really have a lot of options."

"No, we don't." He locked eyes with me for a long moment. "I'll start looking around for another place to live."

What could I say to that? I couldn't ask him to stay in this atmosphere. I sure as fuck couldn't ask him to keep his kid in it.

"What happens if you do move out?"

He tilted his head. "What do you mean?" Then the pieces must have fallen together, because he straightened and added, "Between us?"

"Yeah."

"Fuck, I don't know." He rubbed his forehead and blew out a breath. "I just need some dust to settle so I can figure out which way is up. What happens next, I…. There's no way I can answer that right now."

I nodded slowly. "Yeah, I understand." I wasn't even sure what answer I'd wanted. Part of me hoped like hell we could find a way to see each other once we weren't under the same roof anymore, that we could have something that wasn't strictly platonic or professional. Part of me still heard the echoes of Wes walking out and couldn't stomach the thought of Michael someday calling it quits for those same reasons. Maybe the best thing now was to fix my finances and my shoulder instead of setting myself up to lose someone else when he got tired of being at the mercy of my chronic pain.

I shifted my gaze away from him. "Okay. Well. When you find a place…." I swallowed. "Just, uh, keep me posted."

"I will."

The tense silence lingered for a few seconds. Then he walked out, and I exhaled.

Fuck. Eyes closed, I rubbed the side of my neck, kneading away the spreading tightness.

So that was that. Back to square one. I was once again faced with the prospect of holding up the mortgage on my own, but it didn't induce the same panic it had before. I was worried, but... hell, if I couldn't pay for the house, then the bank could have it and I'd move the fuck on. I was tired of fighting with an account balance for enough peace of mind to sleep at night.

Besides, there was no room in my brain for any of that right now.

Not with the prospect of Michael leaving.

When Wes left, it had been a relief. I loved him, I didn't want him to go, but he took so much bullshit out of this house, the aftermath of our breakup had been akin to recovering from the amputation of a gangrenous limb.

Losing my roommate now meant more than just being saddled with a house and too much debt.

It meant losing Michael. And one way or another, sooner or later, Michael was leaving, and there was nothing I could do to stop him.

And that hurt way more than it should have.

Chapter 17

I FINISHED going over the club's books around three in the afternoon. Earlier, I'd killed some time—anything to avoid the books—auditing the bartenders' nightly inventory. Now there wasn't a whole lot to do besides lock the place up and go home.

Which was certainly appealing, except that Michael would be closing up and heading home soon too. This was one of Daina's custody weeks, so it would only be Michael and me. Just the two of us, which turned the whole goddamned house into a sexual powder keg.

I needed a beer. Beer solved everything.

Well, okay, it didn't solve anything, but spending the late afternoon sitting in the sun with a cold beer beat the hell out of going home and climbing the walls.

Before I left my office, I sent Seth a text. *I'm heading over to the Mountainview Pub. Want to grab a beer?*

A few minutes later, as I was locking the back door, he replied. *Fuck yeah. Got a walk-in, will be there in 1 hr.*

At least I'd have some company.

One beer and ninety minutes later, the usually punctual Seth dropped into the empty chair opposite me.

I made a dramatic gesture of looking at my watch. "What happened to an hour?"

He groaned. "Oh my God. It was—" He paused to flag down the waiter, then faced me again. "A half-hour butterfly on the ankle turned into a ninety-minute-long ordeal."

"Seriously?"

He nodded. "Her boyfriend kept telling her it would hurt, but she insisted that was where she wanted it. And she wasn't afraid of a little pain. So it was about five minutes of tattooing, ten minutes of giving her a chance to catch her breath, five minutes of tattooing, and so on."

The waiter appeared beside us. Seth ordered one of the local microbrews, one even I hadn't heard of. Once we were alone again, he said, "I suggested she let me finish the outline today and then come back later for the shading. No way, she wanted it done today, because this was the last time she was getting inked."

"Now, now, Seth," I said. "Since when are you so unsympathetic with your clients?"

"Since she was keeping me from my beer!"

I smirked. "Okay, fair enough."

Seth chuckled. "All right, so she wasn't that bad, but today was a 'gimme a damn beer' day."

"I know that feeling," I muttered into my beer bottle.

Seth's drink arrived a moment later, and after he'd taken a swig, he said, "So has Michael done anything for you?"

It was only by the grace of God that I didn't wind up with a mouthful of beer in my sinuses. Coughing and sputtering, I stared at Seth. "I... *what*?"

"For your shoulder." He lowered his chin, and one corner of his mouth rose. "What'd you think I meant? His blowjob skills?"

"Right, something like that." I laughed, hoping Seth didn't see any incriminating color in my face. "But to answer your question, yeah, he's been helping a lot. The man's a miracle worker."

"Preaching to the choir."

Of course, Michael hadn't done anything for my shoulder in a while.

Maybe I should get a new acupuncturist. All the treatment without the unrequited lust. That was something else to look into while I searched for a new roommate.

"Jason?" Seth waved a hand in front of my face. "You all right?"

"Yeah." I rubbed the bridge of my nose. "Just... relationship bullshit, I guess."

"What? That fuckwit giving you grief again or something?"

I shook my head. "No, I haven't heard from him in ages." Scowling, I added, "I think he's pretty happy with his sugar daddy."

"Fucker. I swear, he comes back to Tucker Springs, I'm going to tattoo 'douchewaffle' across his forehead."

I snickered. "I'll hold him down for you."

"Deal." He took a drink, then set the bottle down but didn't let go of it. "So what's going on?"

"Nothing a couple more beers won't cure," I said flatly.

"Uh-huh." He adopted his famously ridiculous German accent. "Ze doctor is in. Tell me *all* about it."

I blew out a breath, then pressed my beer bottle against my forehead. "Let's just say I am losing my *mind* in that house."

"Really? I figured Michael would be easy to live with. And his kid's only there half the time."

"Oh, he is. They are." I lowered the bottle. "Dylan's fine. It's Michael."

Seth furrowed his brow. "What? You two don't get along?"

"We do." I shook my head, staring at the table between us. "We definitely do."

"Then…?"

"You know how when you've got a thing for someone, and—"

"Ooh." He grinned. "Trying to live with Michael has got to be, um, hard. He is definitely something to look at."

"Yeah. About that." I picked up my beer again and, right before I took a drink, muttered, "And if I'd been smart, I'd have *stuck* to looking."

"What do you mean?"

"I mean now things are fucking weird." I idly swirled my beer as if it were a glass of wine. With a bitter laugh, I added, "Should've seen that coming."

Confusion deepened the crevices between Seth's eyebrows. "I don't…." Then he blinked. "Wait, *what*?"

And my heart dropped. The bottle in my hand almost did too. "Oh *fuck*."

"You… and Michael…." Seth's eyes slowly widened. "Are you telling me Michael's gay?"

"But, I mean, my son doesn't know. And neither does Seth."

I barely managed to set the bottle down before I dropped it, and I let my face fall into my hand. "Shit. I am so sorry, Seth. I… wasn't even thinking."

"I'm sure I don't have to ask, but you'll be… discreet?"

Michael was going to kill me. Rightfully so too. Fuck, how could I be so stupid?

Seth's chair creaked, and when I looked up, he'd leaned back and turned his gaze away, staring at the ground with unfocused eyes. Disbelief had etched itself into the creases on his forehead. If there was any man walking the planet who could understand why someone might not want to come out, even to a close friend, it was Seth, but he was definitely stunned, and he must've been hurt. And why wouldn't he be? This wasn't something he should have heard from me.

Fuck….

"I am so sorry," I said again.

Seth waved a hand. "It's not your fault. And I'm not, I mean, I'm not angry. A little blown away, I guess." More to himself, he murmured, "I can't believe he never told me."

"Christ," I whispered. "Michael's going to be pissed."

"Look, the cat's already out of the bag. I swear on my life I won't say a word to Michael about it. But, I mean, what's up?" He leaned a little closer, tilting his head. "You guys have a thing going or what?"

"Kind of." Shame twisted in my gut. "We started, then we stopped, then we...." I shook my head. "Fuck, I don't even know."

Seth thumbed his chin. "Have you guys talked?"

"Repeatedly."

He said nothing for a moment, then shook his head. "I don't know what to tell you. I can't imagine living together makes it any easier."

"No," I said. "Not at all. But that situation's kind of resolving itself." I pressed my cold bottle against my forehead again. "Michael's looking for another place. My guess is he'll be out in the next couple of weeks."

"Wow. Damn." Seth drummed his fingers on the table. His tone quiet and with a distinct absence of enthusiasm, he said, "Good luck."

"Thanks."

His lack of advice did nothing for the guilt in my stomach. Seth could usually offer insight like no one else; for a single man, he was wise in the ways of love and lust. But not this time.

We shifted the subject to more comfortable topics, but Seth didn't relax. Whenever there was a pause, his expression turned distant, and whenever he laughed, it seemed halfhearted. I couldn't decide if he was angry, hurt, or trying to absorb the information, and I didn't ask. Call me a coward, but I was afraid to hear how badly I'd fucked this up on top of everything else. Especially with my gut wrapping itself in guilty knots.

After Seth had finished his second beer, he had to get back to the shop to finish a few things before calling it a night. I paid for his drinks, we shook hands, and he left.

As he walked away, I put my elbow on the table and rested my forehead in my hand. A sick feeling twisted beneath my ribs. Yeah, this would simplify matters.

Michael, I really want to sleep with you again, and by the way? I just outed you to your best friend. My bad. So, got any condoms handy?

God. I couldn't believe I'd done this. I didn't even know how to explain it to him without sounding like the inconsiderate jackass I was. I'd seen an opportunity to talk to someone who might understand, to maybe straighten out all this shit in my head, and completely blew Michael's trust in the process. Fuck my life.

How I was going to atone for this, I didn't know, but for the sake of both his sanity and mine, it was a good thing he was leaving. Hopefully sooner than later.

All I knew was, I couldn't keep living with him now that we'd been there, stopped that.

Chapter 18

FUCK. NOT tonight. Please, please, not tonight.

I stared at the ceiling in the darkness as I reached up to rub my shoulder. I had no idea what time it was, and the tightness in my neck dared me to turn my head to look at the clock. Probably one or two in the morning, since I doubted I'd been asleep long.

I should've known this would happen. I'd been restless last night, desperate for something to occupy my hands and mind at work, and I'd unloaded a shipment of booze with the other guys. And rearranged the back room. And generally done way more than I had any business doing.

I closed my eyes and took slow, deep breaths as I rubbed my shoulder gingerly. The pain was deep, as if someone had shoved a knife behind my collarbone and down into my rib cage. Even breathing hurt.

Fuck. Fuck. *Fuck.*

The empty shower called to me from the master bathroom. So did the pain pills downstairs in the drawer beside the refrigerator. Every corner in the house beckoned, promising that euphoric relief that only sufferers of chronic pain could understand.

But if I moved, if I made a sound, I risked waking Michael up. And he'd find me, and he'd insist on treating me, and I wouldn't be able to turn him down because *anything* would be better than nothing, even if Michael's very presence would make me tense up all over again.

I kneaded my neck and shoulder until my hand ached, but it didn't do a damned bit of good. Branches of bright, sharp-edged red fanned out from the first spasm, coiling around my spine, crawling up my neck, creeping toward my other shoulder. Nausea made my mouth water, and I clenched my jaw.

I didn't move. I didn't go get a shower. No pills, no seeking that irrational momentary release from digging my shoulder into a sharp corner.

I'd regret it in a few hours, but I couldn't face Michael.

Not tonight.

All I could do was beg the fucking pain to stop, because God knew *that* had been effective in the past.

It occurred to me that if willing away the pain had ever worked, I never would have met Michael in the first place. Would that have been a good thing? These days, I didn't know. He'd alleviated both my physical and financial pain, but had me lying awake at night for very different reasons, and those reasons were out of his hands and mine. I wanted this. He wanted this. If he didn't, it wouldn't be so goddamned hard for us to stay away from each other.

And now here I was. There he was, at the other end of the house, probably sound asleep behind his closed door across the hall from his son.

"If it's that bad again," he'd said, *"don't hesitate to wake me up."*

"I appreciate the offer, but I doubt I'd ever actually pester you in the middle of the night unless the house was on fire."

"Well, the offer's open. Better that than spending the night bruising the hell out of yourself with a sharp corner."

The offer was there.

And I was in pain.

But I didn't disturb him.

I was still awake when Michael left for work around seven thirty. Now that he was gone, it was safe to put a little more effort into getting rid of this pain than simply wishing it would vacate my muscles.

Drugs. Hot shower. Hot pack. Sitting up. Lying down. More drugs. Another shower. Reheated hot pack. Even the corner didn't help this time; it only made the pain worse without that blissful moment of short-lived relief. *Nothing* helped.

How the fuck was I going to go to work tonight? Shit. I couldn't do my job. I couldn't live with my roommate. I couldn't fucking breathe because of the pain, and the stress, and the... Jesus, every goddamned thing in my life.

"Fuck," I muttered, pressing the lukewarm hot pack against my shoulder. This wasn't good, and if Michael came home, there was no hiding any of it.

If he caught on, he'd ask why I was tense, and I'd either have to slip a bullshit excuse by him or fess up, and that wasn't happening. I just needed to lay low between the time he came home and the time I had to leave for the club. Totally doable. I hoped.

I had just finished with my hundredth hot pack since this morning and was nearing the end of the effective zone for my third painkiller when he arrived. I made a quick escape to my bedroom before he and Dylan came inside.

By nine thirty, I was getting stir-crazy. I needed to get to the club before my employees destroyed the place.

The house had been dead silent for a good hour now. Dylan had gone to bed a little while ago, and Michael hadn't made a sound. I waited as long as I could, making sure they were both settled in for the evening or at least out of sight long enough for me to make a quick escape, and then I left my bedroom.

Stepping carefully and quietly, I went downstairs. A lamp still glowed in the living room, but otherwise this part of the house was dark. I flicked on the kitchen light, grabbed my keys, and—

"Jason."

I damn near jumped out of my skin, which sent pain shooting up my neck and down my arm. Wincing, I turned around to face him as he followed me into the kitchen.

"Michael." I exhaled. "Jesus, you scared the shit out of me."

Arms folded across his chest, he eyed me. "You're in pain, aren't you?"

I gritted my teeth. "I'm fine."

"Don't bullshit me."

I should have known I couldn't hide anything from him.

Avoiding his eyes, I said, "My shoulder's sore. It happens. Don't worry about it."

"Is that—" He paused. "Holy fuck, Jason. You're a wreck, aren't you?"

I resisted the urge to rub my neck. "I'm *fine*."

"The hell you are. I can see it from here." He lowered his chin, eyeing me in that way that told me I wasn't getting away with it. "The only time you keep your arm that protectively against your side is when you're really hurting." He furrowed his brow, shifting his gaze toward my shoulder. "Did you aggravate it somehow?"

Besides stressing myself out? Over physical activity I wish I could be doing but can't?

I cleared my throat. "Define aggravating it."

I thought he might read me the riot act for doing something I shouldn't have when I damn well knew better, but he just chuckled and shook his head.

"And I thought I was stubborn," he said. "All right, what did you do?"

Grinning sheepishly, I said, "Helped unload a shipment of booze at the club."

Michael rolled his eyes. "Really?"

I nodded.

"How bad is it?" he asked.

I swallowed. "It's... pretty bad."

He pointed sharply at the living room. "You know the drill. I'll go get my stuff."

I planted my feet. "I appreciate it, Michael, I really do, but I *have* to get to work." *And I can't do this. Not now.*

"You have a shift manager?"

"Well, sort of. The bartenders who've been there awhile are unofficial supervisors."

"Call in sick." His expression hardened. "Doctor's orders."

"I seem to recall I canceled my appointments, so that's—"

"You want to be in pain all night again?"

I raised an eyebrow. "Again?"

"You don't think I know you didn't sleep last night?" He inclined his head, staring me down.

Swallowing hard, I looked away and shifted my weight. "Sorry if I kept you awake."

"Don't worry about it," he said, his tone gentle. "But don't be a martyr when we both know I can help you." He paused. "Maybe having me as your acupuncturist isn't good for the long term, but tonight…."

Closing my eyes, I released a long breath through my nose. Damn my shoulder. At this point, the pain was worse than the tension between us, and even letting him touch me wouldn't wind me up enough to counter the relief the acupuncture would give me.

Desperate times, desperate measures.

I took out my phone and speed-dialed the club.

"Lights Out, Brenda speaking."

"Brenda, it's Jason."

"Oh, hey, boss. What's up?"

I glanced at Michael and cleared my throat. "Listen, would you mind locking up for me tonight and keeping everyone in line? I need to—"

"Need a night off?"

"I… well, I'm—"

"I've got it," she said. "Don't worry about a thing."

I exhaled. "All right. I'll see you tomorrow night, then."

"G'night, boss. Hope you feel better."

"Thanks." It wasn't until after I'd hung up that I realized I hadn't told her why I wasn't coming in. Even my damn employees knew when I was in too much pain to function. Probably because that was the only reason I ever called out.

No, my shoulder wasn't running my life. Not at all.

To Michael, I said, "All right. I'm off the hook for the night."

"Good. Shirt off, shoes off, on the couch. I'll go get my stuff."

I removed my shoes and, with some effort, my shirt. Like the first time he'd treated me at home, I lay on the couch on my stomach, resting my head on my good arm and keeping the other at my side.

Michael came back with his stuff and sat beside me.

I shivered when his hand made contact with my skin, but he didn't seem to notice. He didn't react, anyway. No, he was 100 percent professional tonight. Dr. Whitman, not Michael. How he could switch back and forth, acting as if we had never been anything except doctor and patient, I'd never understand. We lived together (for now), we were friends (hopefully), and we'd fucked (unfortunately).

But apparently Dr. Whitman had never slept with me.

He tapped a needle into my skin.

I jumped, sucking in a breath. They usually didn't hurt much, but this one stung. "Fuck...."

"Sorry. Is it getting better?"

The initial sting was intense, as was the ache that followed, but after a moment, it eased. "Yeah, it's getting better." I released a long breath.

"Good." He lined up another needle near my neck. "Why didn't you wake me up last night?" He tapped it into place. "No sense being miserable the entire day if you don't have to be."

"You had to work today. I couldn't do that to you."

"But if you're in this much pain...." Michael clicked his tongue. "My God, Jason, I can't let you suffer this way if there's something I can do about it."

I said nothing and let him put the needles in. Some of them hurt, some didn't. Crazy as it was, I didn't mind the sting; it gave me something to think about besides his fingers on my skin. Beggars couldn't be choosers.

Once the needles were in place, Michael left me to relax for a while. In a masochistic, pride-driven kind of way, I almost hoped the pain wouldn't decrease. I didn't want him to be right and for this to be the solution since it was also, indirectly, the cause.

But in spite of my stubborn thoughts, the muscles gradually relaxed. They ached, almost burning in some places, but the bright red claws slowly loosened their grip. By the time he came back, my shoulder was bearably uncomfortable and my neck wasn't full of steel cables anymore. Only the fiercest knots remained, like tiny bullet holes in the center of the muscles.

"The needles will stay in for a few more minutes, but I'm going to try a different technique this time."

"Waterboarding to go with the car battery?"

"Only if this doesn't work." He reached for something on the coffee table. "Besides, I don't have the car battery here, so you're stuck with this."

I glanced back, turning my head as much as my position and the stiffness would allow. In one hand, he had a lighter. In the other, what suspiciously resembled a very large blunt: thin white paper wrapped around some herbs, twisted on one end, but about seven or eight inches long. Had it actually been a blunt—I assumed it wasn't, but what did I know?—it would have made every college kid in town weep with envy.

"I'm not going to touch your skin with it." He flicked the lighter and held it to the open end. "You'll feel some heat, but I won't burn you."

"That's good to—" I sniffed the air and then rested my head on my arm again. "Is that what I think it is?"

Michael laughed as he set the lighter on the coffee table with a quiet *click*. "No, it's not marijuana."

"You sure about that?"

"Yes. And you're not the first to think it, I assure you."

"Does it have any of the same effects?"

"I wish."

You and me both.

"As I said, I'm only going to hold it close to your skin. It won't touch you, so it won't burn." He rested one hand on my other shoulder, and a second later, intense heat warmed the center of the worst muscle spasm.

Instinctively, I tried to draw away from the heat, but Michael's hand kept me still.

"I won't burn you, I promise. Relax."

Closing my eyes, I exhaled and resisted the urge to draw away again as the warmth moved closer to my skin. The heat wasn't unpleasant, but it was close. Similar to the hot showers I took to alleviate the pain—*right* on the edge of too hot.

But relax? Not happening. And it had nothing to do with the smoldering quasi blunt being held dangerously close to my skin. I couldn't draw a comfortable breath with Michael in the room.

The tension in my shoulder started to build again, so I forced myself not to think about the man sitting next to me. I cleared my throat. "So what exactly does this do?"

"It's called moxibustion." His hand moved from my injured shoulder to the side of my neck, and although he continued speaking, the only part of his explanation I caught was something about the heat drawing out toxins. The rest faded into the background, stopping short of my synapses as I focused on the moving, not-quite-burning heat and the comparatively cool presence of his hand on my skin. His voice added to the soothing, almost mesmerizing effect. I might not have understood what he was saying, but Michael's tone kneaded away the tension in my neck and shoulder just like the heat, the needles, and his hand.

Then the heat stopped. Michael's hand left my skin. I blinked a few times, slowly returning to earth.

He took out the needles, dabbing one or two that must have been bleeding a little. When he was finished, he said, "How do you feel?"

"A lot better." I sat up slowly. "Thank you."

"You're welcome. Any time you need it, all you have to do is ask."

"Thanks." I lowered my gaze and reached for my shirt.

"You all right?" he asked. "Besides your shoulder, I mean?"

I closed my eyes. Even thinking about answering sent renewed tension creeping into my muscles. I tilted my head to stretch my neck and shrugged a few times to loosen my shoulders.

"Jason?"

Sighing, I reached up and rubbed my temples. "I'm frustrated." I laughed humorlessly. "Kind of my natural state the last year or two, I guess."

"Anything in particular?" His tone was guarded.

"Just the usual shit. Nothing out of the ordinary." I sighed and pulled on my shirt. "Anyway, thanks again." I started to get up.

"Jason, wait."

His soft voice stopped me in my tracks, and I sank back to the couch.

"Hmm?"

"Is there… anything I can do?"

I chewed my lip. Was this his way of kick-starting the conversation I hadn't had the balls to initiate? The "we're both going to go insane, so to hell with giving me notice—just get the fuck out *now* so we can move on with our lives" discussion?

"Any ideas?" I asked. *Ball's in your court.*

"I can think of a few." *Back in yours.*

"Such as?" *Nope, your turn.*

"You tell me." *Yours.*

I scowled. So he'd kicked off the conversation, but he wasn't going to make it easy for me. Big surprise.

"I don't know if there's anything anyone *can* do as long as we're both still living here. Myself included." I exhaled hard, and the words started coming, fast and furious, on their own. "This is where I get frustrated as fuck. I mean, it's not like I want the whole world, you know? I only want a few simple things that really shouldn't be too much to ask for, and...." I rubbed my hands over my face. "God, I'm sorry. I'm just frustrated. I want...."

Denim whispered across upholstery as Michael shifted on the couch beside me. "What *do* you want?"

Closing my eyes, I rubbed my temples. "Just, you know, a little bit of stability. A little bit of peace. I want my shoulder to stop making my life hell, and I want—" I cut myself off, literally biting my tongue to keep the thought to myself.

His voice was soft as he said, "And what, Jason?"

"Nothing." I lowered my hands and shook my head. "Don't worry about it."

"Jason. Tell me the rest. What was it? What else do you want?"

God damn it, Michael, you know exactly what I want.

I didn't look at him. "You."

He sat up straighter, and though I couldn't face him, I swore I could feel his eyes widening. "What?"

"Are you really surprised?"

He exhaled.

"Not that it matters. Now it's out there." Swallowing hard, I made myself turn to him. "I want you. And I can't bring myself to give a fuck about why I shouldn't. This, what we're doing or not doing or what the fuck ever we're doing, it's driving me *insane*."

Michael moistened his lips. "That's why I'm moving out. It's driving me crazy too."

"I know. And I keep telling myself that." I laughed bitterly and shook my head. "It's probably just as well we're moving on now instead of...." God, just thinking about it hurt.

"Instead of what, Jason?"

I lowered my gaze. "Look, you know as well as anyone what I'm dealing with." I gestured at my shoulder.

"And?" He shifted. "What does that have to do with, uh, wanting each other?"

I met his eyes. "Shut off the doctor side for a minute. Think about it."

He blinked and shook his head. "I'm not following."

"How long would you really want to put up with this?" I rolled my shoulder, pretending it wasn't *already* getting stiff again. "Because it doesn't just run my life. Whoever I'm with, they have to deal with it too." I shrugged with the other shoulder. "That's why my ex left."

Michael's eyebrows rose. "And you think that's why I'm leaving? Because I don't want to deal with your chronic pain?"

"No. No. I... I guess I'm afraid to push for anything because I can't make myself believe it won't fall apart later because of...." I tapped my shoulder.

"Jesus." Michael shook his head. "That's.... I really hope you think better of me than that."

"It's not a question of thinking better or worse of anyone. This is hell for me to live with. I don't expect it to be easy for anyone else to live with it, you know?"

"Your ex was an idiot," he growled. "He obviously had no idea what he had." Michael swallowed. "I can't for the life of me figure out why he'd ever leave, just like no matter how hard I've tried, I can't stop wishing we could make this work."

My heart skipped. I locked eyes with him. "You… you can't?"

"No." He inhaled deeply and took my hand. "I don't even know how much sleep I've lost over this. I want you. Fucked-up shoulder and all."

"Then why…." I curled my fingers around his. "Why *do* we keep fighting it like this?"

He shook his head but didn't speak.

"I know you want to protect your son," I said softly. "And I don't want to confuse or upset him either. But, Michael, Jesus Christ…." I swallowed hard. "You're here too. And, I don't know, maybe you don't want this as much as I do, but if you do, then why are we holding back?"

"You know why we are."

"I know why you say we are." I took a breath, hoping I wasn't treading on thin ice. "But I have to wonder, are you really protecting your son, or are you protecting yourself?" I gestured at the floor above us. "Because the only way he'd ever know is if we took it beyond sleeping together. So the only reason I can think of to avoid this if you want it as badly as I do…."

Michael dropped his gaze. A full minute passed before he finally said, "You're right. It's not only Dylan. Or the fact that you are—were—my patient." He rested his elbows on his knees and combed both hands through his hair. "It's me."

"What do you mean?"

"With you, that was the first time I'd ever let my guard down completely and let myself be what I've pretended not to be for so many years." He slid his hands from his hair to the back of his neck. "And with us living together, it meant going from zero to sixty on a relationship, you know? One minute I'm barely admitting I'm gay." He lowered his hands and looked at me. "The next I'm living with a man whose presence makes it almost impossible for me to breathe."

Speaking of impossible to breathe….

I forced some air into my lungs and was about to speak, but Michael beat me to it.

"You're not the only one who does things to complicate the shit out of his own life," he said softly. "And if we were to…. If things went wrong…."

Cautiously, praying to everyone I could think of that he wouldn't recoil, I reached for his hand. When he didn't, I laced our fingers together. "Do you want to?"

His eyes met mine. "Of course I do."

"Then…?"

He held my gaze.

Then he released a breath and looked down at our hands. "There are so many reasons we shouldn't do this." His thumb ran back and forth along mine. "But right now, I have to admit they're all kind of paling in comparison to the reason we should."

I trailed the backs of my fingers along his stubbled jaw. "And that is?"

He slid his hand into my hair, and a split second before our lips met, he whispered, "Because I fucking want to."

And he kissed me.

Muscles I didn't even know were tense relaxed as Michael's lips met mine. My heart didn't speed up. It slowed down, decelerating from rapid and worried to relieved and calm.

"I am so sick of being responsible," he murmured. "Just once, I want to pretend the rest of the world doesn't exist, and do what I want to do."

"Then why don't we ignore the rest of the world," I whispered, "and take this upstairs?"

"Thought you'd never ask."

Chapter 19

AT THE top of the stairs, Michael hesitated. His eyes flicked toward the closed door behind which his son slept. When he looked at me again, he whispered, "We have to be quiet."

I nodded. "We will be." I drew him in and kissed him lightly. "Don't worry about a thing."

I took his hand and led him to my bedroom, since that put us at the opposite end of the hall from Dylan's room.

Once the door was closed behind us, we were in each other's arms again, and I swore the room vibrated with the desperation that came from being this close to something I'd needed longer than any sane man could live without it. More than once, I had to tell myself this was really happening. Seeing, tasting, feeling weren't believing when I was this sure I was dreaming. That I'd wake up at any moment.

But I didn't wake up, and Michael didn't snap out of it, and with every passing minute, every moment of holding on to him and losing myself in his kiss, this became real. It became real, and my need for him intensified, and we went from grasping clothes to trying to get past clothes.

The need for silence slowed us down, though. We opened every button as if one wrong move might set off lights and sirens. Zippers were drawn down slowly and stealthily. I didn't dare break the kiss, not even to pull in a deeper breath, for fear of making some damning sound.

And when every stitch of distance had been removed, we sank slowly, near-silently onto my bed. My shoulder still ached, the muscles were still uncomfortably tight, but that didn't stop me from running my hands all over him.

He pushed himself up and met my eyes. He slowly ran his tongue across his lower lip, and I wondered if he still had doubts.

No doubts, Michael, I couldn't quite convince my lips to say, so I curved my hand around the back of his neck and drew him into a kiss.

His lips left mine, and he kissed his way from my neck to my chest. As he worked his way farther down, I squirmed and bit my lip, fighting to stay quiet when anticipation threatened to turn me inside out.

"Oh God, Michael," I whispered as his lips inched past my navel. I searched blindly for his hair, and when I found it, I grasped it gently, kneading his scalp because I needed to touch him, needed to hold on to him somehow.

He supported himself on one arm and held the base of my cock in his free hand, and his mouth—oh fuck, his mouth. His tongue drew the most incredible, mind-blowing circles around the head of my cock, teasing me until I was so aroused, my nerve endings were on the verge of igniting. I dug my teeth into my bent index finger, screwing my eyes shut as I forced myself not to make a sound. I held as still as I could, not daring to move, twitch, even breathe, but Michael left me almost no choice as he sucked my cock.

Maybe he was oblivious to how close I was to crying out, maybe he was beyond caring, because he didn't stop. He stroked me with his hand. Teased with his lips and tongue. Moaned so quietly that I was only aware of it because of the spine-tingling vibration against my flesh. Jesus Christ, there was no way this could end without me losing it, and the more he worked my cock as if *inexperienced* wasn't even in his vocabulary, the faster he sent me careening toward that inevitable release.

I bit down harder on my finger, shutting my eyes even tighter. Oh fuck, he was amazing, and I was so close, so damned close, had to be quiet, so close, *don't make a sound, don't make a sound, oh God, Michael....*

The darkness behind my eyelids turned white, and the dam broke. As my orgasm took over, I dropped my palm to the bed, grabbing a handful of sheets, and didn't even have to worry about making a sound because all that pent-up ecstasy escaped my lips in a single near-silent rush of air.

As my vision cleared and my spine sank back to the bed, Michael moved over the top of me. He kissed me, his mouth salty with my semen, and I gripped his hair and the back of his neck as I kissed him harder. I wanted more. Needed more. It didn't matter that I was still coming down from an orgasm, I was so turned on I couldn't breathe.

Fuck me, please, fuck me, my mind screamed as I ran shaking hands through Michael's hair. *Now, please....*

I finally managed to speak, but "Condom" was all I could say. Michael got the message, though. As soon as I said the word, he shuddered, groaning as he pressed his hard cock against my hip.

We sat up but barely stopped making out, breaking away only when we absolutely had to. Somehow—I'll never know how—we got our hands on the condom and lube and managed to put them into place. I smoothed lube onto the condom, squeezing and releasing his cock just enough to make his breath catch, until he grabbed my wrist and stopped my hand midstroke.

"I can't wait," he whispered.

"Neither can I." I kissed him. "Do you want me to—"

"This is perfect." He leaned into me, kissing me again, and used his weight to nudge me down onto my back.

My shoulder blades had just touched the sheets when he broke the kiss and sat up. He ran his fingertips down the inside of my thigh, and I spread my legs. His brow furrowed, Michael guided his cock to me. The coolness of the condom made my pulse jump, as did the heat of his body, and I swore softly as he pressed in.

Jesus Christ, there was nothing more intense than taking Michael's cock so soon after an orgasm. All my nerves were on high alert, hyperaware of everything from his lips brushing mine to his thick cock sliding deeper inside me.

Our eyes met. Immediately my lips tingled with the absence of his, and I reached for him in the same moment he came down to kiss me. I wrapped my arms around him, parting my lips for his tongue and trying like hell to stay conscious as his hips eased into motion.

Groaning softly, Michael slid his arms under me and hooked his hands over my shoulders. His hips rocked slowly, fluidly, pushing his cock into me and withdrawing without so much as a squeak from the bed beneath us. Our mouths moved together, our bodies moved together, and the silence demanded slowness, and the slowness made every motion, every touch, go on forever before the next moment of contact ignited the next nerve ending.

His fingers tightened on my shoulders as his head fell beside mine. A hot breath rushed past my neck. Every muscle in his body—hell, every muscle in mine—quivered from what had to be both exertion and the restraint it took to keep going so, so slowly. The moans he released, warming my shoulder and the side of my neck, were made of equal parts frustration and ecstasy, as if he were a "fuck it" away from thrusting into me hard enough to make it hurt. At the same time, he sounded as delirious as I was from this slow-motion sensory overload.

A shudder drove him deeper. Another arched his spine. Then he lifted himself up on his arms. He threw his head back, his eyebrows pulling together and his mouth opening in a soundless, breathless cry as he pushed his cock deep inside me and came.

His elbows buckled, and the bed creaked softly as he slumped over me. Wrapping my arms around him, I closed my eyes and caught my breath as he caught his.

After a while Michael went into the bathroom to get rid of the condom. We cleaned ourselves up, then carefully eased back into bed as if any creak of the mattress or bed frame would announce to the whole neighborhood that, for the second time, we weren't just roommates anymore.

Lying there together, a sheet draped over us and hands gently drifting over skin that was still hot, we gazed at each other, the air between us electrified with a million things waiting to be said.

So we'd crossed this line. Again.

So here we were. Again.

Now what?

I licked my lips. "Still think this is a good idea?"

Michael smiled, trailing his fingers down the side of my face. "I'm starting to wonder how I ever thought it wasn't."

I laughed quietly as relief brought my heart rate back down a notch. "I've been wondering myself." Turning more serious, I said, "I want you to stay, Michael."

His smile faded. "What if this doesn't work?"

"We'll cross that bridge when we get there. But I can't convince myself it isn't worth a try."

His eyes lost focus for a moment, and then he shook his head. "Neither can I."

I gently clasped our fingers together. "All I ask is, just be patient when…." I gestured at my shoulder.

"I will, under one condition."

I swallowed. "Okay…?"

He brought my hand to his lips and kissed it gently. "Promise me you'll ask for help when it hurts."

I squeezed his hand. "I will. I promise."

Michael smiled. He lifted his head and pressed a soft kiss to my lips. As he settled back on the pillow, he said, "Another thing. If we are going to do this…." He closed his eyes. "Then I need to have a talk with my ex-wife about it."

I grimaced. "How do you think she'll take it?"

"I don't know how happy she'll be. If you thought *my* upbringing was uptight and conservative…." He whistled and then turned to me. "Her parents, mine, Seth's—even if our parents weren't quite as psycho as his, they were all cut from the same fucked-up cloth."

"Do you think she'll try to stop you from telling Dylan?"

He chewed his lip for a moment, then met my eyes. "It's possible. Legally, she can't stop me from doing anything without taking me to court."

"Think she would?"

"I don't know if she would or not. We're on speaking terms, the divorce was amicable, but this…." He sighed. "This could be a bit much for her to take. Hopefully she won't try to keep Dylan from me over it. I'm pretty sure she wouldn't go that far, but you never know."

"Guess we'll hope for the best," I whispered.

Michael nodded. "And if you're okay with it, I'd like you to be there with me to talk to her. And then, assuming that goes well… Dylan."

"Are you sure it's a good idea for him to know we're… what we are? I mean, my mom introduced my siblings and me to my stepfather but didn't tell us they actually had a thing going until she was sure he'd be around for a while."

He watched our fingers lace together between us. "And I agree with that." He swallowed hard, then sat up a little and leaned in to kiss me. "That's why I want him to know."

My breath caught. "You do?"

Michael nodded. "It might be too early in the game to even be thinking this way, but... my gut feeling...." He paused, collecting himself before he continued. "It wouldn't have been this hard to avoid if it was just sex."

My heart beat faster. "No, I don't think it would have."

"And I don't know what it *is*," he said, "but whatever it is, if we're going to do it, then I owe it to my son to be honest. I don't want him growing up thinking gay relationships are strange, and hiding from him is like admitting there's something wrong with us." His fingers went from my face into my hair. "Especially since I think there's a whole lot *right* with us."

"And if things don't work out?"

"Then I'll explain that the same way I'm going to explain this." He broke eye contact for a second but then met my gaze again. "Jesus, Jason, I don't know why I thought I could pretend we were roommates and nothing more." He trailed the back of his hand down the side of my face. "Not with the way I feel about you."

I gulped. "And that is...?"

"I'm not even sure, to be honest," he said. "But I do know I want to be with you, and I want my son to know I'm with you."

And finally—*finally*—my heart could beat properly again.

"That's good enough for me." I put my hand over his and turned my head to kiss his palm. "We already live together. Why rush everything else?"

He smiled, and for the first time tonight, there was nothing tentative or reserved in his expression. Combing his fingers through my hair, he said, "I think I can work with that."

"Good." I pressed my lips to his. "So can I."

As I drew back, though, a knot formed in the pit of my stomach.

"Something wrong?" he asked.

"I, um...." I took a deep breath. "There's something you need to know before we go any further."

"Oh?" He gazed at me intently, waiting for me to elaborate.

"This whole thing has been stressing me out," I said. "So the other night, I was confused. Frustrated. And I don't know, I guess I needed an outlet and maybe some advice."

Michael's brow furrowed, and my stomach knotted tighter.

Wringing my hands in my lap, I went on, "Michael, I'm sorry. I didn't even think about it, and I didn't realize what I'd said until after I did, but I...." I made myself look him in the eye. "Seth knows."

His lips parted. "I beg your pardon?"

"Seth knows. About us." I swallowed. "About... you."

He cringed. Closing his eyes, he sank back to the pillow. "Oh fuck...."

"I am so sorry. I swear, I—"

"It's… it's okay. I know you didn't set out to tell him." He sounded winded, as if I'd punched him in the gut. "He probably would have caught on eventually anyway, but…." Michael chewed his lip. "How did he react?"

"He was surprised. Kind of shell-shocked, I guess. Didn't quite see it coming."

Michael cringed again.

"I feel awful," I said. "I'm used to talking to him about anything, and this time…."

Michael took my hand in his and brought it up to his lips. Meeting my eyes, he said, "I understand. If you've been anywhere near as stressed and confused over all of this as I have, I can't really blame you for talking to him. Wasn't as if you were outing me for spite."

"God, no." I clasped my fingers between his. "I would never—"

"I know." He released my hand and reached for my face. "I'll talk to him. We'll talk to him. He's a reasonable guy."

Smirking cautiously, I said, "Are we talking about the same Seth?"

"Okay, maybe *reasonable* isn't the right word…."

Our eyes met again, and we both laughed.

As my humor faded, I touched his face and said, "So you're… you're really not upset?"

He shook his head. "We'll settle things with him. For tonight, I'm just glad we've settled things with us."

"Me too." I brushed the pad of my thumb across his cheek as I drew him toward me. "Another night of that, I think I might have lost it."

"You and me both." Michael cradled the back of my head in one hand, wrapped his other arm around me, and welcomed my kiss. And that kiss went on. And deepened.

And slowly, silently, with nothing holding us back, we made love again.

Chapter 20

WHEN I finally dragged my ass out of bed at quarter to eleven the next morning, I found Michael in the kitchen, drumming his fingers on the side of a steaming cup of that horror he called tea. He had a shirt on for once, and he looked... nervous?

"You all right?" I asked.

"Yeah. I, um, called Daina on my way home from dropping Dylan at school." He took a deep breath, then released it slowly and met my eyes. "She's on her way over." He gulped. "Would you, um...."

"Do you still want me to be here?"

"*Please*." He rested his hands on my waist. "I could be overreacting. I don't know. I mean, Daina's a great woman, but she *does* share some of her family's views."

"Homophobic?"

"Not necessarily. She adores Seth, but I'm not so sure how she'd feel about Dylan *living* with Seth. Or with me, for that matter, once she knows." Rubbing the back of his neck, he sighed. "God, I have no clue."

I kissed his cheek. "Either way, I'll be here."

"Thank you." He kissed me back, then let me go so I could pour myself some coffee.

As I pulled a cup down from the cupboard, I said, "What the fuck is with you and Daina and Seth all having tight-ass families, anyway? I could have sworn LA was pretty progressive."

Michael snorted. "Oh, the people there *think* they are. Not so much, believe me. Besides, the reason the three of us met in the first place is because our families went to the same church."

"Ooh."

"Yeah. It was actually one of those progressive liberal churches you'd expect in California," he said. "But our families were all insanely uptight and conservative, so they kind of banded together." He paused, sighing. "Mine and Daina's weren't *nearly* as bad as Seth's, though."

"Thank God for that," I muttered. "I don't think families get much worse than those assholes."

"No kidding. I'm definitely not looking forward to coming out to my parents. Not at all." A mischievous grin tugged at his lips. "Now, Daina's parents? I might have to tell them solely for the entertainment value."

I laughed. "You would, wouldn't you?"

"Maybe…."

"Uh-huh."

He chuckled, but then his humor faded. "That's assuming Daina doesn't get upset."

"Do you think she actually will?"

"I'm really not sure," he said quietly. "I keep going back and forth, thinking she'll flip and thinking she'll be fine. If I was only a friend, she'd probably be okay with it. She thinks it's a crime what Seth's family did to him." He paused, reaching up to rub the back of his neck again. "And maybe she'd even be all right with it if we were still married without kids. But with Dylan in the picture…."

"She didn't mind Dylan living with me, though."

Michael lowered his gaze. "She doesn't know you're gay."

I wasn't sure what to make of that. "Oh."

He exhaled. "I should have told her, but I… guess I didn't want to make matters complicated." Laughing dryly, he shook his head. "That worked out, didn't it?"

I had no idea what to say.

"Well," Michael went on, "there's only one way to find out what she thinks, I guess."

"Yeah. I guess there is."

I was halfway through my second cup of coffee and Michael had just put on another kettle of that foul tea when an engine outside turned our heads. It slowed, then idled, then cut off. A second later a car door closed.

"You sure you want to do this?" I asked.

Footsteps outside. Heels clicking on concrete, then hitting the wooden porch with an echoing *thunk*.

"Not much choice now," Michael said. The doorbell rang, and he took a deep breath.

I stayed in the kitchen while he answered the door. The air pressure in the room changed almost imperceptibly as the door opened, then again when it closed. Muffled voices—friendly from the sound of it—murmured in the foyer. Then came the footsteps: the soft sound of Michael's bare feet and the loud, deliberate crack of high heels on a hard floor.

She stepped into the kitchen first. "Oh, hi, Jason. Nice to see you again."

"You too," I said with a difficult smile.

Behind the warmth in her greeting, she seemed uneasy. Whether or not she suspected anything in particular, she must have known there was a reason Michael had asked her here. A matter that needed to be handled in person instead of on the phone.

She eyed me, him, me again, her lips taut and her posture stiff. My continuing presence was a wild card that seemed to unsettle her: Was I part of this? Had I simply not gotten the clue that now was a good time for me to get the fuck out?

She looked at Michael. "So, you wanted to talk to me about something." Her eyes darted toward me, and when I didn't move, she tensed a little more.

"Yes, I want to talk," Michael said. "And I…." He glanced at me, and I gave him a nod that was, I hoped, reassuring. He laid his hands flat on the counter, shifting his weight from one foot to the other. "I needed to talk to you. With Jason."

She swallowed. "About?"

"Well," he said. "I…."

The room fell silent. Beside me, he tapped his fingers nervously on the counter, probably searching for the words. It was all I could do not to give his hand a gentle squeeze, but that would give us away and rob him of his chance to be honest with her about it.

Her eyes flicked back and forth between us, and though she didn't speak, the truth was clearly coming together in her mind. She knew. I could see it in her eyes as she searched mine, then his, then mine again for confirmation. Confirmation I couldn't grant her and that could come only from Michael when he found the words.

Finally Michael put his hand over mine on the counter, and the truth was out. What he couldn't say verbally, he'd declared in that unmistakable gesture. I watched as their eyes met across the narrow kitchen.

Daina jumped as if the contact between our hands had physically shocked her. "What's…." Her eyes again darted back and forth between us. Barely whispering, she said, "Michael, are you telling me you're… *gay*?"

He nodded slowly. Then he said, his voice no louder than hers had been, "Yes. I'm gay."

Her hands searched blindly for the counter behind her, and when they found the edge, she leaned heavily against it, wavering slightly as if her legs had forgotten how to hold her up on their own. After a moment one shaking hand rose off the counter and ran through her hair, and she suddenly looked… lost.

Michael and I exchanged uncertain glances. This was the sinking-in, the comprehending. Lord knew what kind of reaction would follow once the words found their way into her mind.

Evidently confident that her legs would hold her up, she folded her arms across her chest. It didn't appear to be a hostile stance. If anything, she was hugging herself. Bracing herself.

Finally she met Michael's eyes. "How long have you known?"

Michael and I released held breaths in unison. She'd skipped over denial—bypassing "What do you mean, you're gay?" or "How can you be?" or "That's impossible"—and jumped headlong into trying to get her head around it.

He cleared his throat. "I, well." He paused, glancing at me. "Not... not long. I mean, I suspected it for a long time, but I didn't know for sure."

Her eyes flicked toward me again, then fixed on him. "So he's the...." She swallowed. "The first?"

Michael took a deep breath. "I, he's—" He deflated a little, as if the shame had worn him down, and he let out a long sigh. "Yes, he's the first. I kind of knew even as far back as high school, but after the way... after how we were all raised, I was afraid it was wrong. So I tried to pretend it wasn't real."

Daina stared at the floor between us. "But you knew." It wasn't a question.

"In the back of my mind. As much as I tried to tell myself it wasn't true...." He nodded slowly. "Yes, I knew."

She hugged herself tighter, pursing her lips and furrowing her brow. Michael and I exchanged nervous looks again.

His thumb moved across my finger, and Daina jumped again. It was then that I realized she'd been staring at our hands.

Michael pulled his away, glancing at me with raised eyebrows as if to make sure I was okay with it. I nodded. Then he broke the silence. "Daina—"

"Oh my God." She laughed. I couldn't decide if she sounded nervous, relieved, or if it was that humorless laughter that sometimes precedes violent rage. Shaking her head, she added, "I can't believe I didn't figure it out."

"What do you mean?" he asked.

She bit her lip, her focus distant for a second. When their eyes met again, the laughter was gone from her expression, but no anger took its place. "I feel so stupid, I—"

"Daina, please, you couldn't have known," Michael said softly. "I'm sorry, I kept—"

"No, no, it's not that. It's...." She paused, and when she spoke again, she spoke quickly, as if the thoughts were easier to sort this way. "It all makes sense. I mean, I beat myself up for years because I knew something was missing between us. I knew it, but I couldn't figure out what it was, and I felt so guilty. All that time, I thought I was doing something wrong or that there was something wrong with me, and that's why we couldn't connect, and—"

"Daina, you did—"

"Let me finish," she said. "I felt guilty, you know, with the divorce, and Dylan, and...." She locked eyes with him. "But now, now that you've told me this, I know I wasn't doing anything wrong." She paused, her blank expression unchanging for a moment. Then she exhaled and her shoulders relaxed as her lips pulled into a smile. "I wasn't doing anything wrong.

You weren't doing anything wrong. We just weren't meant for each other."

Michael nodded. "Yes, exactly. We couldn't force it to work, and it wasn't anyone's fault that it didn't."

Daina ran her hand through her hair again and laughed. "Michael, you don't even know how much of a weight this is off my shoulders."

"Jesus, Daina, I had no idea...." He reached for her, and she threw her arms around him. The whole world was completely still and silent as the two of them embraced, and when he glanced at me over her shoulder, I smiled at him and he returned it.

After they separated, Michael gestured for us all to sit at the dining room table. We did, Daina and I sitting across from each other with Michael between us.

"So, how did this even get started?" she asked. "I mean, you told me you were moving in with a patient, so...."

"Which was true." Michael laughed softly and glanced at me. "That's how it started. How we intended it to stay."

She released her breath. "I see."

"And I'm telling you now because I wanted you to know," Michael said. "And I won't go behind your back, but I...." His Adam's apple bobbed once. "I want Dylan to know."

She tensed. "You want...."

"I think he should know," he said.

"But...." Daina paused. "He's a little young, don't you think?"

"He was younger when he met Lee."

"Well, yes, I know, but—" She cut herself off, pursing her lips as she stared down at her hands on the table.

"But this is different?" Michael said.

She gave an apologetic nod. "I'm not saying it's wrong, it's…." She looked up, her lips tightening with frustration as if she couldn't find the words. "God, I don't even know. But right or wrong, do you think he'll understand?"

"He will if we tell him. He accepted the divorce, he accepted you remarrying." Michael glanced at me, then back at her. "He can accept this too."

She took a deep breath but said nothing.

"Daina, I understand why you're concerned." Michael kept his voice gentle. "But I don't want him growing up thinking this is unusual or wrong. The way you and I were both raised."

Still silent, she chewed her lip.

"What if *he* is gay?" he said.

Daina's head snapped up, her eyes wide. "What?"

He shifted a little. "If he is, hypothetically, would you want him to grow up thinking there's something wrong with him? The way Seth and I both did?"

She bristled, setting her jaw. "We haven't told him it's wrong, Michael. I'm only suggesting we wait until he's a bit older. Until he'll understand."

"And you don't think it will make him wonder what we think of it if we waited so long to tell him?"

She sighed. "I guess I'm worried about overloading him, I…."

"Daina," Michael said softly, "I want Dylan to know that his father's seeing someone, and I want him to know there's nothing wrong with that. If by chance our son is gay, I don't want him to think it's abnormal." He pursed his lips as if he was trying to decide what to say, but the tautness above his jaw suggested he was simply collecting himself. "I can't be the reason my child has to be confused through high school, ashamed through college, and hating himself until he's suddenly in his midthirties explaining who he really is to his ex-wife."

The shakiness of his voice sent my heart into my feet, and the stunned expression on Daina's face mirrored my own.

She stared at him, lips parted, neither breathing nor speaking.

"I spent twenty years knowing that I was gay," he said, barely whispering. "And pretending I wasn't because I was raised to believe it's wrong. I kept it from myself, from my family, and from you." He laced his fingers between mine. "Whether Dylan turns out to be gay or not, I want him to know it's okay." His voice cracked slightly as he added, "I *need* him to know."

Daina exhaled and shook her head. "Jesus, Michael, I had no idea you went through that."

"No one did," he said. "So do you understand why I want to do this?"

She nodded. "Can… can I at least be there when you talk to him?"

"Of course," Michael said. "I think we should both be there." His gaze slid toward me. "Actually, I think we should all be there."

I ran my thumb along the side of his hand and turned to Daina. "You don't mind?"

She shook her head. "No, I think Michael's right."

"It won't overwhelm him?" I asked. "If we're outnumbering him?"

"No," she said. "This was how we did it when Lee and I were dating. All three of us were there to talk to Dylan. It seemed to work all right." She turned to Michael. "Didn't it?"

"Yeah. Hopefully it will this time too."

Hopefully it would.

AS MUCH as they both wanted to get it over with, it took Michael and Daina a little time to work up the nerve to actually tell their son. Finally, on a Wednesday evening, I went with Michael to pick up Dylan from his mom's. He was quiet the whole way and kept his eyes focused on the road, though he occasionally glanced at me. His hand rested on my leg, and I squeezed it gently, offering what reassurance I could.

I wished there was something I could say to ease his nerves, but I'd been in Dylan's shoes. I was four when my parents divorced, six when my dad remarried, and nine when my mom did. My world had been thrown off its axis every time my folks had sat me down to explain some new development. I struggled to imagine how I would've felt hearing Mom say she had a girlfriend or Dad say he had a boyfriend, and quietly tried to convince myself I wouldn't have been as stunned, jarred, and taken aback as my parents had been when I told them *I* had a boyfriend.

Michael took his hand off my knee so he could steer with both hands as he headed off the freeway.

"You all right?" I asked.

He swallowed. "Nervous."

"You'll be fine," I said. "Just breathe. And don't run us off the road."

He laughed, which at least meant he was breathing, and shot me a playful glare.

A few minutes later he pulled into the driveway of a gray two-story at the mouth of a cul-de-sac not unlike mine. As he turned off the engine, Michael took a deep breath.

"Well," he said, "here we go."

Daina met us at the door. "Hey. Ready?"

"I think so."

"Yeah. Me too." She smiled, though it bordered on a grimace. "By the way, Lee said to tell you good luck."

Michael managed a more genuine smile. "I'll have to tell him thanks later. He's out?"

She nodded. "He took the baby over to his mom's house for a bit. Anyway, come on in. I'll go get Dylan."

While we went into the living room, she went upstairs. We both sat on the couch and exchanged uneasy glances.

Upstairs, a door opened, and when voices trickled down to us, Michael closed his eyes and took another deep breath.

"You'll be fine," I said again, hoping he couldn't tell that I was nervous to the point of nausea.

"I know." He sounded about as certain as I was.

Dylan came into the living room, and both his eyes and his father's lit up. "Hi, Dad!"

"Hey, kiddo." Though I was sure he was still nervous, Michael beamed as Dylan hugged him.

As he let his dad go, Dylan looked at me. "Hi, Jason!" Then he paused, his brow furrowing *exactly* the way his father's often did. "Wait, what're you do-ing here?"

"Dylan!" Daina said, scolding gently. "That's no way to talk to a guest."

His cheeks colored, and he smiled sheepishly at me. "Sorry."

I returned the smile. "Don't worry about it."

"Dylan," his mother said, "why don't you have a seat? We want to have a little talk before you go with Dad and Jason."

Dylan's smile evaporated and his eyes widened. Eyeing us uncertainly, he sat on the armchair, hands tucked under his knees and his feet swinging from side to side behind the coffee table.

Daina sat on the armrest of Dylan's chair and stroked his hair. The three of us exchanged glances, everyone silently prodding everyone else to break the ice and get this thing rolling. I sure as hell wasn't go-ing to do it. The longer the silence went on, the more Dylan fidgeted, and the more I had to struggle to keep from squirming myself. Awkward conversations, with or without children, were not my favorite thing in the world.

Finally Daina took a breath and turned toward her son. She opened her mouth to speak, but he beat her to the punch.

"Am I in trouble?"

"No, no!" Michael and Daina both said.

Michael moved to the edge of his chair. "Not at all."

"You're not in trouble," Daina said. "Dad and I—" She paused, eyes darting toward me. "—and Ja-son just want to talk to you about... some things."

Dylan's feet stopped swinging. His voice was taut with panic when he said, "Is Lee going away?"

"No, of course not," Daina said. "This isn't about Lee and me. He'll be home when you come back in two weeks, same as always."

That relaxed the kid a little, but apprehension lingered in his bunched shoulders.

Michael cleared his throat. "There's nothing bad going on. We just want to... tell you about a few things in case you have any questions or don't understand. Okay?"

Dylan nodded. His feet swung forward this time, first one, then the other, expending that restless energy that makes it impossible for a seven-year-old, especially a nervous one, to sit still. His heels hit the couch with rhythmic *thunks*, echoing my uneasy heartbeat.

Michael and Daina exchanged glances again. She nodded slightly, and he turned back to Dylan.

"You remember when Lee and your mom got together, right?" he asked. "When they first met and started dating?"

Dylan nodded. "Yeah, I remember."

"Okay, well, Jason and I...." Michael paused, slipping his hand into mine. "We're kind of doing the same thing."

Dylan's eyes shifted between his mom, his dad, me, and Michael's and my joined hands. We adults held our breath, waiting for him to say something.

Brow furrowed, he said, "So you have a...." His head tilted slightly. "Boyfriend?"

Michael nodded slowly. "Yes. I do."

"Oh." He was quiet for a moment. I braced against the barrage of questions. How *did* kids react to this stuff? Michael's hand twitched in mine, and I offered a reassuring squeeze.

Finally Dylan spoke again. "Can I have a pudding cup?"

All three of us burst out laughing.

"Of course you can." Daina stood. "I'll be right back." She ruffled Dylan's hair as she walked past him.

While she was in the kitchen, Dylan faced me. "So you're my dad's boyfriend?"

I glanced at Michael, who gave me a quick nod. To Dylan, I said, "Yes, I am."

Dylan's gaze shifted from me to his father and back.

Michael cleared his throat. "So, do you have any... questions? Anything? About this?"

The kid shook his head. A moment later Daina returned with a chocolate pudding cup and a spoon. Michael scowled as she handed it to Dylan, but he didn't say anything.

Dylan shoved the spoon into the pudding and resumed kicking his feet back and forth. After a couple of bites, he said, "Are you guys like Mom and Lee?"

"What do you mean?" Michael asked. "Like, are we married?"

"I guess." Dylan shrugged.

Michael glanced at me. Then he smiled and put his other hand over mine. "Not quite, but we'll see what happens."

"Okay." Dylan looked at me and said matter-of-factly, "My dad's smart. Boyfriends are way better than girlfriends."

"Oh really?" I said. "And why is that?"

The kid wrinkled his nose. "Because girls are gross."

I couldn't stop myself from snorting. Neither could Michael.

"What?" Daina scoffed. "They are *not*."

"Yes, they are!" Dylan giggled.

"Your mom's not gross," I said.

"She doesn't count. She's Mom."

"A seven-year-old's logic." Daina shrugged. "Guess you can't argue with it, right?"

I chuckled. "No, I guess you can't."

"Well," she said with mock indignation, "one day, Dylan, you will realize girls aren't nearly as gross as you think."

Dylan just wrinkled his nose again, and his parents and I laughed. None of us spoke as he continued with his snack, supremely unconcerned by the worries of the adult world.

"All right, kiddo," Daina said when he'd finished with his pudding cup. "Go put that in the trash, and then grab your things so you guys can go."

Dylan pushed himself off the couch and trotted up the stairs.

As soon as the kid was gone, Michael blew out a breath, closing his eyes and leaning back against the couch.

Daina shook her head. "Michael, I think our parents could learn a lot from him."

"No kidding," he said. "That's assuming they ever stop shitting kittens over us not teaching him how evil 'the gay' is."

She made a quiet noise of agreement. "Do they know yet? Your parents?"

"Not yet." He met her gaze. "I think I'll wait on that one for a while. Kind of seems like a 'need to know' thing right now."

"Good point," she said. "How do you think they'll take it?"

"Well, better than Seth's parents, that's for sure."

Daina snorted. "That doesn't take much."

Michael exhaled hard. "Either way, I'll deal with that eventually. I mostly needed you and Dylan to know."

"I'm glad you told us," she said softly.

"Me too." Michael pushed himself to his feet and stepped around the coffee table. He hugged his ex-wife, and for a long moment, he held on to her, eyes closed and pure relief written all over his face.

As Dylan came downstairs, Michael let Daina go, and I stood.

"Ready to go?" Michael asked.

Dylan nodded.

As we headed out to the car, Michael took a breath. "Well, that wasn't so bad. Now I need to talk to Seth."

I cringed.

Michael put his arm around me and kissed my cheek. "I'll sort it out with him. Don't worry about it."

Don't worry about it.

Yeah, right.

Chapter 21

THE FOLLOWING afternoon, we waited for Seth in the patio seating of a pub in the Light District. Nerves coiled in the pit of my stomach, and Michael fidgeted in the chair across from me. I tried to focus on our surroundings, on the gorgeous day we were having, instead of watching the cobbled walkway for Seth.

Summer had definitely arrived in Tucker Springs. The heat wasn't oppressive yet, but it was here, warming my shoulders as I lounged in a metal chair in front of the pub. A couple of bikes whizzed past us. Kids played between the bronze sculpture of jumping salmon and the abstract art fountain.

Apparently oblivious to his surroundings, Michael thumbed the label on his barely touched beer. He wasn't agitated like he'd been on the way to explain things to Dylan, but he was definitely nervous. So much for "don't worry about it."

He glanced at his watch, then exhaled sharply and went back to peeling the label. "You're sure he'll be here?"

I nodded. "You know he will. Assuming he doesn't get tied up with a walk-in client."

"Yeah, that sounds like him."

It took everything I had not to reach for his arm. He was still getting the hang of being anywhere close to out, and knowing our luck, I'd have my hand on him right when Seth showed up. So I kept my fingers wrapped around the base of my beer, which I hadn't touched much either.

Maybe five minutes later, Seth emerged from the thin afternoon crowd. Hands in his pockets, an expression that rivaled Michael's for nerves, he approached slowly, almost cautiously.

None of us spoke until Seth eased himself into the empty third chair with a noncommittal "Hey."

"Hey." Michael kept his gaze down, swallowing hard.

Seth got a waiter's attention and ordered a beer. The silence lingered as the waiter returned and handed Seth a brown bottle.

Once the three of us were alone again, Michael cleared his throat. "So. I guess you already know. About...." He gestured at himself and me.

"Yeah, I do." Seth held Michael's gaze, seeming to search his eyes. "I... I'm curious, though. Why didn't you ever tell me?"

Michael took a deep breath. "Because I wasn't completely sure myself until...." He glanced at me before turning back to Seth. "Until recently."

"But did you think you might be?" Seth asked. "I mean, did this just come out of the blue?" He inclined his head. "Or did you think about it earlier on?"

"Um, well…." Michael swallowed hard. "To be honest? I had some idea before you came out to me."

Seth exhaled. "I figured."

"You did?"

Nodding, Seth said, "About the time Charlie Turner joined us in band? Hell yeah."

Michael's mouth fell open and his face colored. "You knew about that?"

Seth laughed softly. "Come on. You weren't exactly subtle."

Michael laughed too. "Man, I didn't think anyone knew."

"Well, I don't think Charlie ever caught on."

"Thank God for that." Michael set his shoulders back and looked Seth in the eye. "So we're clear, I wasn't out to hide anything from you. I thought about telling you. God, I don't even know how many times I thought about that."

"So why didn't you?" Seth's tone was gentler than I'd ever heard it before. "What did you think I would do?"

"It wasn't you. I didn't want to say anything because I didn't want to accept it myself." Michael reached for my hand. "And I didn't fully accept it until recently."

Seth stared at our hands for a long moment. "I can respect that. I really can, because coming out…." He whistled. "Not an easy thing to do. And it was a bit of a surprise, but hey, if you guys are happy together, then I'm happy for you."

"You're not upset that I never told you?"

Seth's normal response would have been made of snark, but there wasn't a trace of sarcasm when he spoke. "Michael, if you weren't ready to tell anyone, who am I to hold that against you? I, of all people, know how hard it is to come out."

"I know," Michael said, "which is what worried me. You trusted me enough to tell me, but I couldn't return the favor?"

"It's not a favor." Seth leaned forward, folding his arms behind his beer. "You didn't owe me anything. Yeah, I hope you can trust me with things like this, but did you trust yourself with it?"

Michael straightened, lowering his gaze. "I…. Maybe that's it."

"Course it is." Seth picked up his beer. "I'm never wrong, you know that."

Michael laughed again. "Oh, how could I ever forget?"

"No doubt." Smirking, Seth brought his beer up to his lips. After he'd taken a drink, the seriousness returned to his tone. "I mean it, Mike. Honestly. You had to figure it out on your own, and when you were ready, I would have listened." His gaze slid toward me. "Or when your boyfriend was ready, as it were."

My face burned, but Michael squeezed my arm, and I relaxed.

Then, to Seth, he said, "Yeah, you're right. I needed a few years to really get it through my head."

"Well, no one ever accused you of being a fast learner." Beat. They both laughed, and Seth said, "Don't worry about it, man. Seriously."

"Thanks," Michael said. "I think."

Seth chuckled. "I'm not all that surprised you're gay, to be quite honest. I'm really not. But there is one thing I really, really do *not* get."

"And that is?"

Seth picked up his beer and gestured toward me with it. "What the *fuck* is up with your taste in men?"

Michael snorted, and I laughed aloud.

"Love you too, Seth," I said.

"I'm just saying." He shrugged. "If you were worth dating, I'd have gone after you myself a long time ago."

I rolled my eyes. "Yeah, okay. We've been over this before. You're not my type and I'm not yours."

"Exactly." He raised his beer in a mock toast. "Hence my assessment you're not worth dating."

"You're a real pal, you know that?"

"Don't take it personally," Michael said with a smirk. Winking at me, he added, "He'd change his tune if he knew some of the things I know."

Seth stared at him, speechless for once. Then he shuddered. "God. I don't even want to know."

"Liar," I said into my beer bottle.

He flipped me the bird, and Michael and I snickered.

"So how does Daina feel about all this?" Seth asked. "With Dylan living with you two and all?" He paused. "Did *she* know you were gay?"

"She didn't know." Michael shook his head. "But she does now, and she's cool with it."

I chuckled. "And Dylan sure approves."

Seth's eyebrows jumped. "Does he, now?"

"Yeah. Boyfriends are better than girlfriends."

Seth blinked.

"Because according to him," Michael deadpanned, "girls are gross."

Seth threw his head back and laughed. "Are you serious?"

"Hand to God," I said. "I witnessed the whole thing."

"Well, shit." Seth set his beer on the table. "He could write the marketing slogans for that mythical gay agenda." He made a sweeping gesture in the air as if he were outlining an imaginary sign. "Go gay, because girls are gross."

Michael choked on his beer.

"I think I should tattoo that on both of you," Seth said. "Banners across your chests. On the house."

"I'll pass, thanks," I said.

"Me too." Michael smirked. "No tattoos for me anyway. I hate needles."

Seth and I both eyed him incredulously.

He showed his palms. "What?"

The three of us laughed, and then Michael held up his beer bottle. "To supportive, understanding friends."

Seth raised his. "Even when those friends have god-awful taste in men."

"And even worse taste in tattoo artist friends," I said, clinking the neck of my bottle against theirs.

"Hey, fuck you." Seth took a drink, and as he sat back in his chair, he gestured down the road leading toward his shop. "You know, Mike, that office space across from Ink Springs is still available."

"Is it?" Michael tapped his beer bottle against the edge of the table, his gaze drifting toward the same road. "Hmm. I might have to check it out." Then he looked at me, and the corner of his mouth rose. "It *would* give me a shorter commute."

I smiled. "That's true, it would."

"And," Seth said with a grin, "I wouldn't have to drive clear across town for my appointments, since you'd be right across the street."

"Aha!" Michael smacked his arm. "I knew there was something Seth-serving in this."

"Well, yeah." Seth shrugged. "What'd you expect? Altruism?"

"From you? Please."

I nodded. "What he said."

Seth waved a hand. "Yeah, yeah, fuck you both."

"So, about that office space," Michael said. "As long as we're down here, why don't we go have a look?"

We finished our beers, paid our tabs, and left the pub's patio.

And as we strolled across the busy town square toward the place that could one day become the new Tucker Springs Acupuncture clinic, Michael laced his fingers between mine.

I glanced at him and smiled, curling my fingers around the back of his hand. It was hard to say where this would go. We'd done things completely out of order: moving in together, then sleeping together, then figuring out that what we had was worth all the headache such an arrangement could bring. But I'd never been one to do things the easy way, and Michael seemed content to wander down this unbeaten path with me, crooked as it was.

It was too soon to call it something as complex as love, too late to call it something as simple as lust.

But as we walked hand in hand from the town square toward Seth's shop in the heart of the Light District, I was happy. Life wasn't perfect. My shoulder wasn't completely fixed. All my stress hadn't magically evaporated. My club wasn't miraculously a profitable, well-oiled machine.

But I had Michael. And we were happy.

I brought our hands up and kissed the backs of his fingers, and Michael smiled. I returned it, and as I lowered our hands, we kept walking.

Maybe my fucked-up shoulder hadn't ruined my life after all.

L.A. WITT is an abnormal M/M romance writer who has finally been released from the purgatorial corn maze of Omaha, Nebraska, and now spends her time on the southwestern coast of Spain. In between wondering how she didn't lose her mind in Omaha, she explores the country with her husband, several clairvoyant hamsters, and an ever-growing herd of rabid plot bunnies. She also has substantially more time on her hands these days, as she has recruited a small army of mercenaries to search South America for her nemesis, romance author Lauren Gallagher, but don't tell Lauren. And definitely don't tell Lori A. Witt or Ann Gallagher. Neither of those twits can keep their mouth shut....

Website: www.gallagherwitt.com
Email: gallagherwitt@gmail.com

READ WHAT HAPPENS NEXT IN
TUCKER SPRINGS

SECOND
HAND

A TUCKER SPRINGS NOVEL
HEIDI CULLINAN
MARIE SEXTON

Second Hand

By Heidi Cullinan and Marie Sexton
A Tucker Springs Novel

Paul Hannon flunked out of vet school. His fiancée left him. He can barely afford his rent, and he hates his house. About the only things he has left are a pantry full of his ex's kitchen gadgets and a lot of emotional baggage. He could really use a win—and that's when he meets El.

Pawnbroker El Rozal is a cynic. His own family's dysfunction has taught him that love and relationships lead to misery. Despite that belief, he keeps making up excuses to see Paul again. Paul, who doesn't seem to realize that he's talented and kind and worthy. Paul, who's not over his ex-fiancée and is probably straight anyway. Paul, who's so blind to El's growing attraction, even asking him out on dates doesn't seem to tip him off.

El may not do relationships, but something has to give. If he wants to keep Paul, he'll have to convince him he's worthy of love—and he'll have to admit that attachment might not be so bad after all.

CHAPTER ONE

GOING INTO the pawnshop was a mistake. I knew it the same way I'd known two months before that Stacey was going to leave me—some nagging sense of unease deep in the pit of my stomach. On the day she'd left, I'd stopped on my way home and bought dinner because a little voice in the front of my brain chattering away like a chipmunk refused to believe that sense of impending doom. It insisted that chow mein and sweet-and-sour pork would make Stacey smile and everything would be all right.

The chipmunk had been silenced by the empty house and the note on the bedroom door.

The chipmunk, however, never learned. Today my inner rodent had prattled on, reminding me Stacey's birthday was in two days. I couldn't not get her a present, it reasoned, not after all the time we had together. Worse, how could I pass up a chance to win her back?

Of course, I was looking to buy said present at a pawnshop. This was new desperation, even for the chipmunk.

I opened the door of the pawnshop but stopped dead in the doorway when I got a good look inside. The neon lights outside flashing BUY—SELL—PAWN should have tipped me off as to what kind of atmosphere I'd find, but I'd never actually been in a pawnshop, and it was far worse than I'd antici-pated. It was dirty and cluttered and sad. Discarded items—mostly TVs, stereos, and Blu-ray players—lay dead on the shelves. An entire wall held musical in-struments, silent in the absence of their owners. The smell of cigarette smoke and something else lingered in the air—something I couldn't identify. Something that reeked of failure. I was overwhelmed by the same sense of helplessness I felt at the animal shelter, all the animals behind bars, wondering why nobody loved them anymore.

Jesus, Paul. Is this really the best you can do?

I almost turned and walked back out, but the man sitting behind the counter watched me, his booted feet on the glass display, a half-smoked cigarette drooping between his lips.

"Can I help you?" he asked, and I marveled at the way the cigarette stayed stuck in the side of his mouth.

I shoved my hands deep into my pockets. "I'm looking for jewelry."

He took the butt out of his mouth and smiled at me as he stood up. "You've come to the right place, my friend."

I doubted that, but I chose not to contradict him. The "right place" would have been the jewelry store down the street, its windows full of gold and diamonds, but I sure as hell couldn't afford that. One of the downtown art galleries had beautiful glass pendants, but the chipmunk had protested. They were colorful, but twisted glass wouldn't win Stacey back.

The owner led me around the shop through a faint haze of cigarette smoke, past glass cases full of iPods and cameras, GPS navigators and laptops, to one along the back wall that held jewelry. The selection was crazily eclectic. Giant turquoise bracelets and dainty gold chains, wedding bands and strings of pearls.

"You looking for anything in particular?" he asked.

That was a good question. What should I buy? Not a ring. I'd already given her one of those. Never mind that it was currently sitting in a bowl on my bedside table. Not a bracelet. She didn't like them because they got in her way when she worked.

"A necklace?" I asked.

"Don't sound so sure of yourself." He stuck what was left of the cigarette in the side of his mouth, squinting against the ribbon of smoke that rose past his eyes as he unlocked the cabinet and began to pull out the displays of necklaces. Cigarette smoke curled around the coarse twists of his hair.

"Are you allowed to smoke in here?" I asked.

He glanced up at me, almost smiling. His black hair was shaved short on the sides and in the back, but the top was longer, spiked straight up in a way that hinted more at laziness than style. He was one of those casually cool guys, I realized, who were naturally put-together and suave, who found everybody else slightly amusing. And slightly stupid. "My store."

"Yeah, but aren't there city ordinances or something?"

He took the butt out of his mouth and leaned both hands on the edge of the glass counter to look at me. He was taller than me. Thin, though. Not bulky at all, but he still managed to make me feel small. "Pretty sure I'm the only honest pawnbroker in town. As long as I'm not fencing, cops don't exactly care about my personal vices."

"I see." I tried to hide my embarrassment by look-ing down at the necklaces.

"Is this for your mom or a girlfriend?"

"Girlfriend," I said, deciding he didn't need to know about the *ex* part of the equation.

"In that case, I'd say stay away from pearls and Black Hills gold." He shrugged and rubbed his hand over the close-cropped dark hair at the nape of his neck. "They're sort of old-school. Opals too."

"She likes sapphires."

"Show me a woman who doesn't." He knocked the cherry off his cigarette onto the concrete floor and rubbed it out with his foot. He tossed the butt in the trash can behind him before turning back to me to point to a necklace in the center. It had a stone so dark blue, it was almost black. "This is the only sapphire I have right now, but if you want my opinion, it sort of screams 1995. Now this...." He pulled a necklace hanging on a black velvet display stand out of the case and set it on the glass in front of me. "This one's new. Platinum's all the rage, you know."

"Platinum?" I touched the necklace. It looked like silver to me, but I wasn't exactly an expert on jewelry. The stone appeared to be a large rectangular diamond surrounded by a bunch of smaller round ones. "It looks expensive."

"*Looks* being the operative word." He smiled and crossed his arms. "The platinum's real, but the diamonds aren't."

"They're fake?"

"Cubic zirconia. Just as pretty, but way more affordable than the real thing."

I wasn't sure about giving Stacey imitation stones, but it was definitely the nicest necklace he had. Even used, it was more than I could really afford, but that chipmunk in my brain was enamored with it, positive it was the only thing Stacey would want.

"I can pay you half in cash and half on my card. Is that okay?"

"No personal checks, but cash and credit both work."

"Do you have some kind of nice box or something it can go in?"

He laughed, revealing perfect teeth that seemed extra white against his bronze skin. "No, I'm gonna give it to you in a Ziploc baggie." I wasn't really sure what to say to that, but he laughed again. "I'm kidding. Yeah, I got a box around here somewhere. You think I'm running some kind of second-rate establishment here?"

The way he said it, it wasn't a challenge. He seemed to be mocking himself more than anything, admitting that of course this was a second-rate store.

That was, after all, the entire idea of a pawnshop. Second owner. Second hand.

I hoped very much that in my case, it would mean a second chance.

CHAPTER TWO

EL WATCHED the necklace-buyer leave, trying not to laugh at the absurdity of it all. The whole thing had *long-term disaster* stamped all over it. Sometimes his customers were desperate. Sometimes stupid. This one? Mostly he'd seemed perpetually confused.

When his cell phone rang, El found he was still smiling, thinking about Clueless Joe as he answered. "Tucker Pawn."

"Aren't we all bright and cheery this evening?" Denver Rogers's voice was rough, full of drawl that didn't quite come from the South. "If my ears don't deceive me, you might actually be smiling. You take someone home and get snuggly last night?"

"I don't snuggle."

"Well, something's got you sounding like Suzie Sunshine."

El smiled at the image of the necklace-buyer as Suzie Sunshine. Oddly, he kind of was. "Just a customer."

"Oh?" There was a world of innuendo in that single syllable.

"*Just* a customer." Brownish-red hair, pale skin, little freckles across his nose. El couldn't help but imagine the soft white skin in the places that didn't see the sun. "He was damn cute, though."

Denver whistled through his teeth. "Well, goddamn. Somebody call the *Tucker Gazette*. Emanuel Mariano Rozal is showing signs of humanity. Next thing you know, he might settle down and start collecting cats."

"Whatever."

"So we on tonight, or what?"

"Looks like *or what*."

Denver's huff betrayed his irritation, and El could picture him scowling. The two of them had a weekly "date" at the Tucker Laund-O-Rama, which wasn't nearly as exciting as it sounded. It had nothing in the world to do with romance and everything to do with having somebody over the age of twenty-two to talk to while their socks ran the spin cycle.

"What is it this time?" Denver asked.

"I told Rosa I'd watch the kids."

"Come on, man. Your entire fucking family, and she picks you?"

"Miguel's on call for the fire department, and his wife can barely deal with their own kids. Rosa's fighting with Lorenzo's wife—"

"About what?"

"I'm doing my best not to know." If there was one thing El had learned, it was not to get involved in family drama. Especially when it came to the women. *Especially* when it came to his little sister Rosa, who made the stereotype of the fiery Latina woman look like Shirley Temple. "She's been leaving them with her neighbors, but they got busted for possession—"

"Nice."

"That leaves Abuela, and she's too old to have to deal with those little shits on her own."

"What about your mom?"

Leave it to Denver to notice the person El had left off his list. "Look, man, it's me. I said I'd do it."

Denver sighed. "Someday you're going to wake up and wish you'd gotten out from behind that counter a bit more."

"And you're going to wish you hadn't bulked up on 'roids." El was pretty sure Denver didn't actually use steroids, but when a man was built like a fucking barn, he could take a bit of ribbing.

"Why can't you bring the kids along?"

"You serious?"

"Why not? They might liven things up a bit."

El thought about Rosa's three kids running around the laundromat. They'd scare away any little frat boys in a heartbeat, no doubt about it. "You're on. Eight o'clock?"

"Sounds good."

"Hey, Denver?"

"Yeah?"

"I don't snuggle."

He laughed. "Fine. But I take back that 'signs of humanity' remark. You're as much of an asshole as ever."

EL HAD thought he was watching the kids because Rosa had to work, but when he showed up at her house at six thirty, he found her wearing tight black jeans and high-heeled boots and displaying a whole lot of cleavage. Not exactly the sort of thing she'd wear to wait tables, not even at Giuseppe's.

"Christ, Rosa. Put on a sweater or something."

She hooked her hands under her breasts and lifted them a bit. "Fuck off, bro."

"You didn't tell me it was a date."

"You didn't ask."

True enough. The fact was, the less El thought about what his sister got up to, the better. He was sure the feeling was mutual. "Who is he this time?"

She turned away to study her hair in the mirror. "Somebody I met."

"No shit, Captain Obvious. Where at?"

"Out."

He sighed and sat down on her couch. "You got three kids by three different dads, and not one of those sperm donors is worth a damn. When you gonna learn?"

"Just because you don't date doesn't mean I can't." She pinched her cheeks and reached for a tube of lipstick. "I ain't cut out to be a nun."

Which meant El was a monk. Which wasn't entirely off the mark, which annoyed the hell out of him. "Do you ever stop to think about where you're going and what you're doing? Do you ever think of the future? Your kids' future, maybe with a stable male role model in the picture?"

She bared her teeth at him in the mirror. "Oh, but sweetheart, if they need a male stick-in-the-mud, they can look to Uncle Emanuel." She yelled down the hallway, "Let's go, kids. I got places to be."

"And men to do," El said under his breath.

The only acknowledgment El received came in the form of a middle finger flipped his way.

"WHAT DO you care that she's on a date?" Denver asked El two hours later as they loaded clothes into side-by-side washing machines.

El glanced around to make sure Rosa's kids weren't listening. They weren't. They were running around the laundromat, playing hide-and-seek among the tables and chairs. The only other person around was a young woman wearing skintight sweatpants with Greek letters across her ass. She had on headphones and was handily ignoring the world.

"It's not that it's a date," El told Denver. "It's that she's being an idiot."

Denver slammed the door to his washer and glanced sideways at El as he thumbed quarters into the machine. "You're the most judgmental person I know."

"It's not my fault people are stupid."

"Am I included in that assessment, Mr. Genius?"

El sighed and slammed his own washer shut. "Look. When she's hurt and crying because another loser has left, she comes clean and tells me what she really wants. She says she wants a nice guy who'll settle down with her. Take care of her and take care of the kids. Come to family dinners and help Abuela when she needs it. Somebody who'll be part of the family."

"Makes sense." Denver shrugged and glanced down at the floor, his voice gruff as he added, "Nothing wrong with wanting that."

"I'm not saying it's wrong. But look at it this way: you work at Lights Out. Biggest, gayest club in town, right?"

"Yeah."

"And you're standing here saying you wouldn't mind finding somebody to settle down with, right?"

Denver's jaw tensed and he took a step back. "I never said—"

"My point is, you have a couple hundred gay boys to pick from every night. But you don't."

Denver relaxed a bit, probably because he knew El wasn't about to hound him on the settling down thing. "Club's nothing but college boys looking to get laid."

"Exactly." El turned away to put his money into the slots. "Men in the straight clubs are no different. She meets these guys at the bar, takes them home within a week, then wonders why they turn out to be losers."

"Where's she supposed to meet them?"

"I don't know. PTA meetings. Church. The grocery store." El waved his hands to indicate the walls around them. "The fucking laundromat."

Denver snorted. "I take it she don't go to those places?"

"She does, actually, and guys ask her out, but you know what she says? She says they're old or they're fat. Or maybe they're going bald. So she keeps choosing these drunken asshats at the bar, then wondering why they don't turn out to be Mr. Right."

"You think Mr. Right's hanging out at Tucker Laund-O-Rama?"

Of course, when he said it that way, it sounded pretty stupid. "Maybe. Yeah."

Denver raised his eyebrows. "Do me a favor, El. Let me know when he walks in the door."

CHAPTER THREE

WHEN I got home after work, I found a bright pink flier wedged into the rickety screen on my front door. I left it on the kitchen counter while I dialed Stacey's number.

No answer.

I found myself staring at the flier. *Curb Appeal Contest*, it read. Although houses in similar neighborhoods in Tucker Springs were in high demand, my little corner, an older section tucked away between the edge of the Light District and the railroad tracks, was slowly falling into disrepair. The self-appointed homeowners association was always trying to come up with ways to increase property value. Block parties. New playgrounds. It seemed this time it was a drive to improve the look of the lawns and houses in the neighborhood. I was about to toss it aside when the bottom line caught my eye. *$500 cash prize.*

I could use five hundred dollars. No doubt about that.

I dialed Stacey's number again. Still no answer.

I put on some music and stuck a frozen dinner in the microwave, wondering how much it would take to win the contest.

Our secret judges will be patrolling the neighborhood, looking for yards that are well-kept, colorful, and inviting.

That didn't sound too hard. And for a cash prize—

There was a dull *pop*, and the kitchen went dim and completely silent.

"Goddammit." I shoved away from the counter and glared at the faded wallpaper as if I could bore through to the wires beneath. "Should have known."

I'd long suspected the wiring in the house had never been up to code and that whatever work had been done on it hadn't exactly been on the level. The annoyances of living in a place where half the wiring consisted of duct tape and extension cords were part of my daily life. No running the microwave and the window-unit air conditioner at the same time. No using the computer while watching TV. Every time Stacey had used her blow-dryer in the tiny master bathroom, it had caused the lights in the bedroom to flicker and my alarm clock to blink incessantly until I reset it.

With a weary sigh, I went into the garage and flipped the breaker. Back in the kitchen, I turned off the AC and restarted the microwave, then went back to the flier.

The contest would run for a month. They even had a website where weekly scores would be displayed. It was worth a shot, right?

I called Stacey again. This time she picked up. "Hello?"

She sounded annoyed, and my heart sank. "Hey, Stacey. Happy birthday."

"Paul, you shouldn't be calling. I've told you that. If Larry finds out—"

"Well, I certainly wouldn't want to upset your new boyfriend," I said, unable to keep the bitterness out of my voice.

She sighed. "What do you want?"

This definitely wasn't going the way I had hoped. The microwave beeped, signaling that my dinner was ready. Why hadn't I waited until afterward to call?

I took a deep breath. "I wondered if you're free tomorrow night? I wanted to take you out to dinner for your birthday. We could—"

"I can't, Paul."

"It's only dinner."

"I don't think I should. Larry wouldn't like it."

"I'm not asking Larry. I'm asking you. Come on, Stacey. After seven years together, I'm not even allowed to wish you happy birthday?"

"You just did. And I appreciate it. But dinner isn't a good idea."

I opened the microwave door, waving away the steam. "How about lunch, then?"

She sighed, and I felt certain she was about to give in. "Coffee?"

"I don't know, Paul. I—"

Whatever she said after that, I didn't hear, because my smoke detector went off, loud and high-pitched, obnoxious in a way only smoke detectors could be.

"*Shit*. Hang on, I'll be right back."

"Paul? Are you okay?"

I put the phone down and tried to figure out how to make the noise stop. I couldn't reach the smoke detector on the ceiling, but I took off my shirt and waved it at the thing, jumping up and down, trying to scatter whatever hint of smoke it thought it smelled. The damn thing went off about every time I cooked, whether I burned anything or not.

"Shut up," I yelled at it. I swung my shirt again and it caught the edge of the lid and pulled it open. The incessant whine of the alarm stopped, although my ears were still ringing.

It hardly seemed fair that Stacey had picked the house and then left me to deal with it, although if I had my way, she'd be coming back.

"Fire alarm again?" she asked when I picked up the phone again. "Hasn't the landlord fixed that yet?"

"Of course not. Listen, Stacey, couldn't you at least meet me for a cup of coffee?"

"I don't know."

"Please?"

She sighed. She was relenting.

"Just coffee," I emphasized, jumping into the small window I saw opening for me. "How about after work tomorrow?"

It took her a moment, but she finally said, "Fine. Coffee. I can be at Mocha Springs at five."

I'd have to skip out of work early, but I'd figure it out. "Great. I'll see you then."

She'd already hung up the phone.

I'D ALWAYS wanted to be a veterinarian, but that wasn't how things worked out. Instead I was a glorified receptionist at a veterinary office. On the bright side, my boss, Nick Reynolds, was a great guy.

"Hey, Doc," I said to him the next afternoon. "Is it okay if I cut out a bit early today?" Normally on Thursdays we closed the office at five, and I'd be there another half hour or so wrapping things up, but I didn't want to be late for my date with Stacey.

Nick was in his early thirties, only a few years older than me. He was successful and handsome and built. I suspected he had women throwing themselves at him. "How early?"

"Maybe quarter to five or so?"

He shrugged. "Yeah, I think I can manage." He tossed the patient file he'd been reviewing on my desk and leaned back with his elbows on the counter behind him. The motion stretched his shirt tight across his chest in a way that would have made many a coed swoon. "You got a hot date?"

I looked down at the file so he wouldn't notice me checking him out. Nice chest. Tattoos up one arm. He was attractive and funny and nice, and that made him intimidating as hell.

Not that I was gay or anything. I just happened to notice he looked nice.

"I'm meeting Stacey. It's her birthday."

He didn't say anything, and when I looked back up, he was shaking his head. "You're a glutton for punishment."

"I just think—"

"It's cool," he said, turning to pick up the next file on the stack. "I don't mind you leaving."

"Thanks, Nick."

He glanced over at me again. He raised his eyebrows and opened his mouth as if he were about to say something, but then the bell on the door rang and his next client came in.

"Hey, Seth," Nick said, reaching across the counter to shake the man's hand. He nodded at the pet carrier the man held. "How's Stanley?"

"Fatter than ever."

Nick laughed. "Somehow I'm not surprised." He motioned to the door that led to the exam room. "Go on back. I'll be with you in a minute."

Once he was gone, Nick turned to look at me. He had insanely blue eyes. Almost as blue as Stacey's. "Listen, kid, it's not my business, but if you want my advice on Stacey—"

"I don't."

Because I'd heard it before. I was better off without her. She was bad news. Move on.

He sighed. "Okay. Fair enough. I guess in that case, I wish you good luck."

"Thanks, Nick."

He shook his head as he turned to leave the room. "God knows you're going to need it."

LAST MECHANIC STANDING

L.A. WITT

A Wrench Wars Story

Everyone at Jim Irving's garage is gung ho about *Wrench Wars*, a new reality show featuring mechanics. Everyone, that is, except talented mechanic Chandler Scott, the sole employee who has refused to sign the contract. The rest of the mechanics are pressuring him too, because without Chandler—and his volatile interactions with his boss—no one's getting on the show.

Chandler's one ally is Jim's son, Mark, who's being forced to work for his dad until he pays down his student loans or finds a better job—and who's been Chandler's secret lover for a while.

Then a playful tryst in the garage blows up in their faces, giving the network ammo to blackmail Chandler by threatening to out Mark to his father. Now Chandler is backed into a corner, and Mark needs to decide how far he's willing to go to protect the man who's been sharing his bed… and may have stolen his heart.

www.dreamspinnerpress.com

WRENCHES, REGRETS, & REALITY CHECKS

L.A. WITT

WRENCH WARS

A Wrench Wars Story

When Reggie's garage became part of a popular reality show, business went through the roof. And he supposes having his shop in the black is a fair trade for jumping through the network's hoops.

As the show's lowest-ranking producer, Wes is tasked with proposing a new spin-off show to Reggie. The sexy mechanic makes him sweat on a normal day, but this time, Wes is holding cards he can't show. With execs breathing down his neck, he's expected to pitch a show Reggie will never agree to do, even if his rejection puts his existing show on the line.

The network is counting on Reggie refusing to sign. But they're not counting on their messenger falling for the man they're trying to fire.

www.dreamspinnerpress.com

Rules of
Engagement

L. A. WITT

Dustin Walker has no idea that avoiding the search for Mrs. Right could send him into the arms and bed of Mr. Right Now. According to Dustin's mother, he should be out looking for his next wife so he won't be the divorced black sheep of the family. Instead, he passes his free time at a local bar and pool hall, where he meets someone who's everything his ex-wife wasn't: funny, caring, faithful… and male.

Is Brandon Stewart just Dustin's way of getting over a bitter divorce? Can Dustin really care for him, or is it simply that Brandon is the complete opposite of his ex-wife? Dustin keeps their affair as quiet as possible, because if it continues, he knows he'll eventually have to come out to his homophobic family or walk out on the man he's trying not to love.

www.dreamspinnerpress.com

Sequel to *Rules of Engagement*

Brandon Stewart and Dustin Walker started dating two years ago after meeting in the local bar over a game of pool. Dustin has struggled to come out to his homophobic family and come clean about his relationship with Brandon, and now they're planning to get married. Now, in a bid to fix broken ties, Dustin's brother Tristan is trying to reconnect with him, which makes Brandon wonder if he, too, can mend fences with his own estranged brother. But is sixteen years of silence long enough for old wounds to heal?

www.dreamspinnerpress.com